ROMANCED BY THE MOUNTAIN MAN
COURAGE COUNTY CURVES

MIA BRODY

This is a work of fiction. Names, characters, places, and incidents either are the product of the author's imagination or are used fictitiously. Any resemblance to actual persons, living or dead, events, or locales is entirely coincidental.

Copyright © 2023 by Mia Brody

All rights reserved. No part of this book may be reproduced or used in any manner without written permission of the author except for the use of quotations in a book review.

1
BLADE

"Have you ever shot someone's eye out with one of your arrows?"

I glance at Jacob, the eight-year-old kid that's currently holding his compound bow and arrows. The boy is Duke's younger brother. Since his father abandoned the family, Duke has been struggling to care for his brothers and his sick mama. The mountain men of Courage County have taken the family under our wing.

Now I'm at the outdoor archery range that's part of the gym on the edge of town. I'm supposed to be showing him how to shoot. I think there's something deeper the guys expect me to teach him, but I know fuck all about how to be a decent human.

"No," I answer, my voice coming out deep and

rumbly. It's a voice that earns me a nice living. These days, I'm a book narrator, reading dirty romance novels out loud. It's not a bad way to make a paycheck, but that's not why I do it.

"Oh." He looks disappointed at the fact that I've not blinded anyone with my archery skills.

Fuck, is this the place where I'm supposed to discourage him from being violent? If so, the other men really picked the wrong mentor for the boy. I grew up fighting for everything I had.

He continues his questioning, "Could you if you wanted to, even with one arm?"

"Yep." As soon as the word leaves my lips, I know it was the wrong thing to say. After losing my arm in the service, I spent some time searching for a hobby. I saw a video about an armless man who could do archery, and I figured I could do the same. Turns out, I'm good with a bow and arrow.

Jacob's eyes light up, and I worry he's already trying to decide on a target.

"But just because you can do something doesn't mean you should," I add to the end as if that will make a difference. If the kid is anything like I was at that age, it's too late. The idea is already in his brain.

"But it doesn't mean I shouldn't," he argues back.

Fuck, this kid is me. Better to stop while we're

ahead and everyone still has their vision. "We'll do another lesson next week."

He groans but gathers his gear away without too much complaint. While he's doing that, I check my phone for a new message. There are a few emails about my projects, including a couple from two other authors I read for. I'm developing an excellent reputation in the industry even though I'm new to it.

But there's only one name I'm scanning my inbox for: Gwen Hughes. She's my favorite writer and maybe I have a small thing for her. Very tiny. Barely noticeable. Seeing her name in my inbox never makes my mouth go dry or my heart beat fast. I don't obsessively watch those live videos she does for her fans like some damn creeper with his hand crammed down his pants. Nope, totally normal over here.

She hasn't messaged me again. Not since yesterday morning when she sent me one to say she had a book signing in Asheville today. Like I didn't already know that. Like I hadn't already talked myself out of meeting her in person three times.

I don't have another message from her since I didn't respond to her invitation. She asked me to meet up and I just ghosted her. Because I'm an asshole.

It's better this way, I remind myself. Better if she doesn't know me. I'm no romance book hero. I'm not one of those devilishly handsome alpha wolves or the sexy fated mate that seduces the beautiful curvy woman.

I'm the bastard who's done whatever it took to build a good life. One where I can eat real food from my own garden instead of searching through the dumpsters for old, spoiled remnants. One where I can go to sleep at night on a soft, comfortable bed instead of whatever springy, lumpy mattress was reserved for foster kid of the week.

Yeah, she's better off never knowing me. Hell, it's not like she could find me anyway. She might remember that I live in Courage County. But other than a small group of fellow mountain men, no one here knows my legal name and that's what I use when I'm narrating. To the fine folks in town, I happen to be Blade. A name that doesn't encourage people to get too close, which is just the way I like it.

"How many people have you shot with your arrow?" Jacob asks as the two of us start down Main Street toward my truck. I promised his brother I'd bring him home tonight. I figure it's one less thing for Duke to worry about this way.

"Zero."

"Are you sure?" He asks as if I'm holding out on him. "My brother says you were in the Army. That means you had to have shot somebody, right?"

I don't bother correcting him that I was in the Navy or disappointing him with the knowledge that I didn't shoot anyone. Instead, I help him into my truck and start a conversation with him about the latest superhero movie he saw at the theater in Sweetgrass River last weekend.

He chats a mile a minute, starved for attention and affection. I barely have to grunt out a response before he starts up again. By the time we're at his place, he's educated me on the complexities of all his favorite superheroes. I promise I'll see him next week and wave as he disappears into his house.

With a tired sigh, I begin the drive to my cabin. It's a forty-minute trip up the mountain. Forty minutes to think about Gwen, to wonder where she is and what she's doing.

Did her book signing go well today? Did lots of her fans show up and gush about her latest book? Fuck, I hope so. I hope she's happy. I hope she's not thinking about me and wishing I were by her side the way I'm wishing that.

She's single. I've been able to put that much together, but it doesn't mean that she spends her nights dreaming of me the way I do of her. It doesn't mean that she wakes up in a cold sweat under twisted sheets and has to touch herself to be able to relieve the insistent ache.

Until about three years ago, I'd never read a romance book in my life. I rarely read anything until I lost my arm. The days in the hospital were filled with endless appointments involving physical therapy and mental health counselors followed by circle time where a bunch of guys got together to bitch about their lost limbs.

But at least, the days were busy. Nights were the worst. In the sterile, dark room there was nothing to distract me from the phantom pain.

Then a local women's organization gave out baskets filled with gifts for the injured veterans. The second-hand reading tablet was inside of mine. Guess whoever donated the reading tablet didn't think to erase it.

I picked it up when I was trying to distract myself. I found the device pre-loaded and opened a book on it. That night was my first taste of a story from Gwen Hughes and well, I've been a fan ever since. I own all of hers in print. Both the paperbacks and the hardcover editions with discreet covers.

Hell, I have an entire shelf of my bookcase

devoted to her works. I just wish it contained the signed copies. It sounds crazy, but I want to hold something she's held. I want to sniff the books to see if they have the slightest hint of her perfume.

Now all of my wishes have caused me to start hallucinating. That's the only explanation for the woman standing by the broken-down car with a hand on her curvy hip. Her long, brown hair flows down her back, and she scowls at the smoking sports car.

It takes me a full thirty seconds to realize that I just passed her. I've never been one to leave a motorist stranded on the side of the road. Definitely not a woman alone. But there's an awareness in my gut, something is tingling.

"It's not her," I say out loud as I put the truck in reverse. I'm seeing things. I'm so damn desperate to know what it feels like to have my hands on her hips and stare into that captivating brown gaze that my imagination is in overdrive.

She's the only reason I started narrating. Once I was hooked on Gwen's books, I started watching her live streams. From there, I knew I had to find a way to get close to her.

When I saw she was looking for a male narrator for her books, I sent her an email. I insisted I was the man for the job. I didn't tell her that I had no experience or that I spent hours watching video tutorials to learn how to do it after she decided to give me a chance. I just needed to be around her.

Now, I stop on the side of the road, and the woman turns. That scowl that was directed at her car is focused on me.

My heart skips a beat. *It's her.*

Gwen Hughes is actually on my mountain, and she looks mad as hell too. She pushes her hair out of her face and marches up to my truck. With every step, her little blue jean skirt is swishing against those thick thighs that are a staple in all of my dirtiest fantasies. "Would you believe some asshole sold me this piece of junk?"

2
GWEN

"Out of all the ideas you've had, this has to be your craziest," I tell myself as I turn off the interstate and onto the exit. I know from the GPS system in my car that Courage County is nearby.

The rural town sees some tourists for its old-fashioned charm but it's not like Charleston, South Carolina where I'm from. Thousands of tourists flood our city every year, and I love that. Tourism helps the local businesses, and it's fun to meet new people.

"Maybe it'll turn out well though." I've been reading a book on self-compassion, and it encouraged me to talk to myself the way I would a friend. Right now, I'm trying to channel my friend and fellow writer, Zoey Hart. She always has something cheerful to say to me. She's my biggest supporter, but I don't know how she'd feel about this little detour.

I was supposed to be on my way back from a book signing in Asheville. If all went well, I'd be home in just a few hours. Instead, I'm taking the scenic route. Yes, the scenic route involves driving through Courage County. It's the place where *he* lives. My book narrator.

OK, most authors hire a narrator when they start creating audiobooks. If they happen to write a book with a hero and heroine falling in love, then they would need male and female narrators.

I was trying to save money in the start and read out the heroine's parts which meant I only had to find a hero. My narrator was an unknown when we began working together. I took a chance on him, and he took a chance on me. Now, we've read three books together over six months. Plenty of long nights repeating dirty words to each other.

Oh, Landon Shaw is never anything but professional with me. Sometimes, there's a slightly flirty tone to our messages and once, I thought maybe he was trying to figure out if I have a boyfriend. But there's nothing between us. Absolutely no reason for me to go visit him. Except that I have to.

I can't explain it, and this is going to sound a little bit ridiculous, but I think he's my soulmate. No, scratch that. I *know* he is my soulmate. Deep in my gut, there's a knowledge that I'm meant to be with him.

I'm not sure he feels the connection just yet. After all, I invited him to my book signing today but he didn't show up. He didn't message me back after that. Maybe going to see him after his clear sign that he's not interested is a little weird. Maybe it even borders on stalking. But I'm pretty sure Landon is just shy.

He has social media accounts for his book narration services, yet he's never posted a picture of himself. He just has a sterile logo for his avatar. His posts are all about the books he's read and the authors he's working with. There's absolutely nothing personal.

He let it slip once in a private message that he lives in Courage County, North Carolina. That explains the delicious Southern drawl he has. That combined with his deep, raspy tone makes it sound like his voice is whiskey mixed with gravel.

I hit a pothole on the side of the road, startling

me from my thoughts about the sexy book narrator. My companion in the backseat meows.

"I know, I know, I'm sorry," I apologize to my cat.

He was adopted from the shelter after I learned he had no more time left on his stay. I couldn't let anything happen to him. My parents would flip if they knew I had an animal for companionship. They're leading professors at a prestigious university and believe that everything should have a practical purpose. Things exist to be studied and understood, not to bring beauty or joy or companionship.

The GPS unit powers down without warning. The stupid thing has been cutting off on me all day.

I glance at the dashboard, fighting a wave of frustration when I see the temperature gauge is rising again. I splurged on this car a few months ago. I told the salesman I wanted a fast car. Apparently, I should have specified that I also wanted one that works properly.

Still, I might be able to make it into the town. Right now, I'm near mountains. I know from an earlier search online that there are mountains in Courage. So, I have to be close to the area, right?

There's a hiss, and steam begins pouring from under the hood. I fight back a string of curse words and gently guide the car onto the side of the road.

Stupid sports car. Stupid me trying to be whimsical and fun.

"Should have been practical about this," I mutter as I get out of the vehicle and stare at the steaming mess. That's what my parents would have told me. That's what they've told me my whole life. If they had it their way, I'd be spending my days in a classroom, instead of doing what makes my heart beat fast, which is writing my dirty romance books.

I pull my cellphone from my oversized purple bag. No reception.

For the first time since I started this journey, I wonder if it was meant to be. Maybe I'm not meant to find my soulmate. Maybe I'm meant to be alone with just my cat and my book boyfriends for the rest of my life.

While I'm lost in my musings, a truck goes by. The sleek black vehicle doesn't even stop for me. *So much for small town friendliness.*

As soon as I have the thought, the truck stops as if the driver heard me. Slowly, the vehicle reverses, and the passenger window rolls down.

I push my wild hair back from my face and march up to the truck, indignation running through me. It's late in the day and it'll be hours before I can get the roadside service out here, which means I'm stranded. "Would you believe some asshole sold me this piece of junk?"

The ignition cuts off, and a man emerges from the truck. The first thing that catches my attention are his eyes. They're so brown, they're almost black. His dark hair is cropped close on top, reminding me of those military haircuts. But his short beard definitely isn't standard issue. His black t-shirt stretches tight across his shoulders and clings to his chest.

He gestures toward the steaming pile of metal with one hand. That's when I realize he's missing an arm, or part of it at least. It stops just above where his elbow would be. There are tattoos and scars, though the scars seem newer than the tattoos. It makes me curious about how he lost his limb. "Want me to take a look?"

Oh, I'd love for him to take a look at a whole lot of things, the least of which is this disaster of a financial decision. I'd much rather he do a thorough inspection of my body. As if he's reading my thoughts, his gaze travels over me. I have an overwhelming urge to tug my too-short skirt even higher, to tease him with a glimpse of what he could have.

His look feels like a caress, warming every part of

my body. That place that only tingles when I write the sexy scenes in my books tingles now.

No, bad Gwen. There's only one person that should be giving me those tingles and it's him. My soulmate. Not a random stranger on the side of the road who raises his eyebrows as he waits for my answer.

"Do you know anything about cars?" I ask him. Maybe this kind stranger will fix the car and send me on my way to Landon. Then during our wedding, he can be a special guest. He'll read out a speech about how he knew we were meant to be. Alright, I'm a romance writer. I'm always imagining a happy ending.

"Enough that I boosted them way back when." He pauses and runs his hand affectionately over the bright yellow roof. He lets out a slow whistle, a sound that I don't normally think is sexy but with him, it somehow is. "You got a beauty."

"If only she ran," I point out with a grumble. In his speech, I'll be annoyed but charming. He'll think I looked like the cute but somewhat flighty beach girl from the city. Landon will laugh along with the description and put his arm around my shoulders. He'll squeeze me tight and smile, his eyes filled with the kind of love I've only ever written about.

The mysterious stranger moves around the front of the car. He carefully raises the hood so as not to get burned. He ducks his head when it's safe and peers into the engine area. "What are you here for anyway?"

"My boyfriend lives around here," I answer, the lie rolling off my tongue far too easily. OK, I'm not so far gone that I believe Landon Shaw is my boyfriend. But I'm out here on a deserted area of a freakin' mountain with a man I hardly know. It seems like the smart thing to do is to let him think that someone will miss me if I disappear.

He peers around the hood, taking me in again. "Is that right?"

"Yes," I answer, nodding vigorously. "So, it would be a bad idea to make me disappear."

He grunts and stomps back to his truck where he grabs a toolbox. He brings it back, sets it on the ground, and clangs around under the hood.

"Your radiator is shot," he finally calls. "I can pour some water in. Then I can follow you in my truck to the local garage. Got to warn you though. They aren't likely to have the parts in stock for a car this expensive."

My shoulders slump, but I remind myself to be plucky. That's how I want him to remember me in his speech. Will he mention my lie about the boyfriend in it? Then again, I guess it doesn't matter. Landon will understand. He'll find me delightful and quirky.

He moves to the back of his truck and produces a gallon of water from the back seat. He holds it up. "Or maybe we should call your boyfriend. We could wait right here for him together."

I swear there's a smirk on his face, like he knows I was lying. But that's impossible. This stranger doesn't know a thing about me. Unless he recognizes me. Not that Mr. Sinfully Handsome looks like the type to pick up a romance book, but you never know. Romance readers are a diverse group and even men enjoy them.

I put my hands on my hips and study the car. I pretend to think it over before I turn again to Mr. Handsome. Then I glance at the watch I'm wearing. "He's in the middle of work right now. I'd hate to disturb him so if you don't mind…"

"We could wait a while and then call. I don't have any plans for the rest of the day."

Before I can figure out how to get out of this situation without admitting that I'm a liar, my baby meows. Relief fills me. Of course, the perfect excuse. "I don't want to keep my cat waiting. We've been on the road all day, and he's starting to get anxious."

For a moment, I think he's going to say something more, but he licks his very plump, very biteable bottom lip. "Then we'll get to the garage, and you can call your boyfriend from there."

3
GWEN

"Yes, I know it's a bad idea to lie to the scruffy mountain man," I tell my cat. "Your mama is setting a terrible example for you today."

At least, I can acknowledge this as I chug along the road into Courage County. I glance in the rearview mirror, making sure the hulking black truck is still behind me. There's something about this big man's presence that has me all confused. I should be focused on Landon. Getting to Landon is what matters most.

When we arrive at the auto shop, the mountain man approaches a dark-haired woman at the front of the shop. He speaks to her in low tones before nodding to my car.

I don't know why seeing him talk to another

woman annoys me so much. I've never been the type of woman that needs to be the center of attention, but I find myself irrationally jealous of anyone else he talks to. I want this big mountain man focused only on me.

The woman steps around the counter. She's wearing baggy, blue coveralls with Gabby on the stitched nametag. She follows us outside.

"I definitely won't have the parts in for this thing." She sends me an apologetic look and focuses back on the car. She peers under the hood and the fact that she's more into the vehicle than she is my companion eases a little of the jealousy burning a hole in my gut.

The sky is already turning to dusk. In my original plan, I would find Landon and he would be so enthusiastic about seeing me. We'd go out for dinner and then I'd crash at a local motel. Except I haven't seen any motels in this town. "Where am I going to stay tonight?"

"Well, you could call your boyfriend," the man suggests. "I'll loan you my phone."

"I don't know his number off the top of my head," I lie. Screw it, I'm not inviting him to the wedding. He'll be that character that mysteriously disappears off the page, never to be seen again. With that decision, I confess the truth, "And maybe I let you think there was one when there wasn't."

A smug look crosses his face, and I instantly regret telling him this. "So, then you need lodging for the night."

"The bed and breakfast is closed," Gabby calls from under the hood. She doesn't even look away from the car. "The Andersons had a pipe burst. Whole place is flooded."

"If only there were a Good Samaritan nearby…" My mountain man shakes his head, feigning regret.

I narrow my eyes at him. I'm not sure if he's trying to get me to ask for help or if he's needling me.

Gabby pokes her head out from my hood and says, "I think the nearest place is probably two hours up the road."

My shoulders slump. I'm grimy from traveling all day, and I'll have to get a taxi to take me back to Courage tomorrow. Still, all of this will be worth it when I get to meet Landon. He'll love me on the spot, I'm sure of it. "Do you happen to know where it is?"

"It's a hostel outside of Asheville," Gabby volunteers. "I've crashed there a couple of times. It's co-ed."

"That could be new," I say more to myself than anyone else. I've never been in a co-ed dorm. I went to college for a year, but it was an expensive one my parents wanted me to attend. They cared more about looking good in front of their academic friends than what I wanted.

"You're not staying at a fuckin' hostel. You'll stay at my cabin." The grumpy giant is scowling down at me like this whole thing is my fault. OK, so I made a bad decision buying from that used car salesman. But the radiator thing isn't my fault. Neither is getting stranded in this ridiculously small town. *Why hasn't my book narrator found me yet? Can't he sense that I'm nearby?*

I put my hands on my hips and try to match the giant's glare. "You can't just make decisions for me, you bossy grump."

He blinks, unaffected by my half-hearted insult. "Place isn't safe. My cabin is. End of discussion."

Gabby slams the hood. "You were right on the money about the radiator. It'll be about two days before I can get a replacement. The good news is the engine likely isn't damaged."

She turns her attention to me. "The hostel can be kind of sketchy, sometimes. Depends on who's there. Definitely not my favorite place."

Sketchy isn't my thing. Not after the day I've had. I drop my hands from my hips and scowl back at the mountain man. "Do you have space for my kitty?"

He smirks, and I realize too late what I said. "I'd love to meet your kitty."

"What do you mean you're about to go to the cabin of some guy you don't know?" Zoey hisses into the phone.

I'm in the bathroom at the garage. I called her to let her know what was going on. She used to live in South Carolina too. We got started writing books about curvy women around the same time. Except that she went on vacation in Lake Tahoe and fell in love with Sheriff Brock. Now they live there together with the world's most adorable baby.

"I'm telling Brock."

Brock took away my bestie from me. But it's kind of hard to hate him when he adores her so much. He's always doting on her and loves to spoil her. All Zoey has to do is look at him, and he'll do whatever she asks.

"He'll check out the mountain man and make sure he's not a religious weirdo or worse, one of those people who don't eat sugar." I can practically hear her shuddering. She has a major addiction to her sweet treats.

"It's fine. He's fine. I'll only be here for two days," I reassure her. I haven't told her the real reason I'm in town yet. I didn't want her thinking I'm crazy or feeling sorry for me.

"You'll still make it to the taping, right?" She asks. In just a few days, I'm supposed to be featured on *Mornings with Maddy*. It's the most popular daytime talk show in the country, and Maddy is going to be interviewing me about my books. I've written two dozen wolf shifter romances. They're books about humans that can shift into wolves. Usually, it's the hero that's the shifter. But sometimes, the heroine is one too.

"I'll make it to the taping," I reassure her. I started self-publishing my books, just putting my books online for fun. Slowly, they became popular and last month, I signed a lucrative movie deal, one of the largest in recent history. There are already predictions my series is going to be the next big thing, and my agent is fielding calls for foreign rights, merchandising options, and more.

"And you have your pills," she prompts.

"Yes, I do." Thyroid disease means not only do I

have a curvy figure, but also that I have to take daily medication to keep my hormone levels balanced. Zoey worries about me. She's the one who noticed I was getting sluggish and acting moody all the time. She insisted I see an endocrinologist. Thanks to her prodding, I feel better than ever.

She sighs. "Alright, I want you to check-in by text every few hours. If you miss even one check-in, I'm having my big, sexy husband send in the FBI and CIA and maybe even the SWAT guys. They're hunky too."

I seriously doubt that a small-town sheriff holds any sway with the national agencies but before I can point this out to her, I hear a low growl in the background.

"Oops," she murmurs, and I already know what happened. Brock overheard her describe the SWAT guys as hunky. He's possessive in the best way and won't even let another man glance in her direction. I love that about him, the way he's so determined to keep my bestie safe. He lives for her and their daughter.

I wish her good luck and tell her I love her before ending the call. I use the bathroom then check my reflection in the mirror, grimacing. I look so damn disheveled. Good thing I'm not meeting Landon just yet.

I wonder if the owner of Hotel Grump knows who Landon is. Ooh, maybe he does. Maybe they're good friends and he'll introduce me to Landon in a totally not obvious way, so I don't look like a crazed stalker.

When Landon does learn who I am, we'll have a good laugh about it. That will be the story that the mountain man tells at our wedding. Yep, that will be a much sweeter ending. But if I want to have my happy ending, first I have to get to know the bossy grump outside.

After I leave the bathroom, I sign a few sheets of paper for Gabby and give her my credit card number. Then it's not long before I'm on the road with the grump himself.

"Where do you live?" I ask after we've been in silence for a few minutes. Why is this man so quiet? Doesn't he have all these words bubbling up inside of him that just have to be shared or he'll explode?

"The mountains."

I wait for him to ask me a question because that's what you do in polite conversations. The other person is at least supposed to feign interest in you, except that I don't think this man will even bother pretending. "What's your name?"

He hesitates for a second too long. It's the tell that he isn't being truthful with me. "Blade."

"That's not really your name," I scoff.

"And you didn't really have a boyfriend," he reminds me. "So, why are you here in a little place like Courage? It's not like we're a huge tourist attraction."

I can feel my cheeks flush. At least, it's dusk outside so the cab isn't very light. "The GPS unit in my car is malfunctioning again."

He makes a noise of disbelief in the back of his throat. "Is there anything truthful you can tell me?"

I huff out a sigh, surprised by how well Blade can read me. It's Landon that's supposed to be able to do this. It's Landon that should know how to read my moods and figure out how I really feel. "My name is Gwen, and I'm here to find my soulmate."

4
BLADE

"Your soulmate?" I repeat in the too small truck cab that now smells like her. My heart is pounding. How could my Gwen be here looking for her soulmate?

"You don't have to say it like that," she argues, but there's a quiet note in her voice. She doubts herself or at least, this mission. Good. I don't want her with some other man. No one else should get to touch those luscious curves or kiss her cherry red lips.

"You believe in that non-sense?" I know she does. She has to if she spends her days writing about women that find their very own happy endings. Fuck, I want that for her. I want her to be happy and to know love and desire. But no one around here is good enough for her.

"I'm a romance writer. It's one of the side effects of the job. I always believe in the happy ending." Her cat meows beside her as if confirming what she said. He's in a carrier between us on the seat, a plushy one with comfortable cushions and what looks like a fluffy blanket.

"Yeah, but why are you looking for your soulmate here? Do you just move from place to place in search of him?" I've watched her videos. She lives in Charleston. She lives in a sunny little beachfront property, and she writes regularly at a café down the street from her home. She's never mentioned travel in the videos. But surely, she's not here for me. She can't be.

"Can I tell you a secret?" She asks before continuing on anyway, "You're going to think this is really dumb. But there's this guy. He narrates my books, and I think—no, I know—we're meant to be. We're soulmates even though I don't know all that much about him. I do know he lives here. Any chance you know a Landon Shaw?"

I'm quiet for a long moment. If there were ever a time to take a chance and confess my true identity, this would be it. But soulmates don't actually exist. Happy endings don't happen, and guys like me don't get to keep the beautiful ball of sunshine that bounces into their lives. "Name doesn't ring a bell."

"Well, do you think it would for someone else in town?"

"Unlikely." My friends are the only people that know what I do, and they wouldn't bring that up in casual conversation.

"Oh," she sighs out the word.

Her disappointment hits me straight in the gut and for some crazy reason, I want to fix this for her. I want to find a way to give her the soulmate she's looking for. "Why do you want to find this guy so badly anyway?"

"Don't *you* want to find your soulmate?"

And disillusion some poor woman against the whole idea of love and marriage? No thanks with a capital no. I'm sure as hell not a saint, but I've never broken a woman's heart either. Still, I search for a soft answer, something that won't hurt the beauty beside me. "Sometimes, being alone is a good thing."

"Yeah," she answers with a sniffle.

Fuck, fuck, fuck. She's crying. Gwen is sitting beside me, and the girl is crying over not finding her soulmate. A soulmate that I can't possibly be. I clear my throat, uncomfortable with her emotion.

"You know, I could help you look for him while

you're here." The words leave my mouth before I even think them through. What the hell am I going to do? Am I going to parade her around in front of every single male in town and get each one to admit that he's not Landon Shaw?

Yes, yes, I am. But I'll be by her side the entire time so none of these fuckers get any bright ideas. Then by the time her car is fixed, she'll be convinced Landon isn't here and she'll move on with her life. Probably find some other bastard to be her soulmate instead. The idea has me gripping the steering wheel so hard my knuckles ache.

"You would do that for me?" She asks with a little bit of hope in her voice and fuck, the sound is killing me.

All of those nights listening to her read out the dirty parts of her book in that sensual voice and now she's here. She's right beside me, and she has no idea who I am. No idea of how many times I've fisted my cock and called her name.

"Sure." The word comes out strangled.

She claps her hands together in excitement, the sound loud in the cab of my truck. "Can we start first thing tomorrow morning?"

I grunt out a non-comital response, but she's too excited to be paying much attention to me. How do I get myself into these dumb ass things? How can one woman's tears affect me this much?

"How will we start our search?"

With liquor. Lots of liquor. That's what it will take to get me through the next few days. Oh, sure I could try to win her over. I could tell her I'm Landon. I could romance her. But what would that get her? A broken heart, that's what because I'm no woman's prize.

Still, her books got me through a dark time in my life. I owe this to her and if I can find a way to give her just an ounce of the sunshine she's given me, I want to offer it. "What do you know about the guy?"

"Hmm...well, he's got a sexy voice, so I'll know it when I hear him!" She says this with such a note of triumph, but all I can fixate on is the fact that she thinks my voice is sexy. Sure, I know women like it. Her audiobooks get a ton of positive reviews for my voice, but knowing she finds it sexy does something to me. It makes my chest puff out with pride.

"So, you're telling me you'd recognize his voice?" I work to keep mine normal, trying not to give it away. "But let's say for argument's sake that you don't recognize it, what else do we know about him?"

"I think I would recognize my soulmate's voice,"

she argues. "But I know that he lives here in Courage County. He loves the color honey. I don't know what that's about."

Honey is the exact shade of golden brown that her eyes are. It became my favorite after I saw her first author photo.

I turn the truck onto the winding dirt road that will lead to my cabin as she says, "He'll know about alphas and fated mates too."

I make a mental note that I can't afford to let on that I know all about shifter romances. They're love stories where one or both of the love interests can also shift into an animal. A popular trope in the genre is that each shifter has a fated mate, one person that they were meant to be with. 'Which are…?"

"I write shifter romances, mainly wolves. Although bears are becoming popular. I can kind of see the appeal after…" She stops herself.

I'm desperate to hear the rest of that sentence. I'm fascinated by how she does her work, and I have a million questions I want to ask her now that she's here. But I push them down and remind myself that I can't be obvious. "So, we have a guy that knows about wolf romances. Got it."

She blows out her breath. "It's not much to go on.

But then, maybe he'll recognize me. Do you think that could happen? I'll totally let you be part of the wedding ceremony. I was going to write you out, but I think you're a pretty cool guy."

I stop the truck in my driveway and turn off the ignition. I don't say anything for a long moment, processing. She has a lot of words. This shouldn't surprise me, given what she does.

There's no way in hell I'd sit on the sidelines and let her marry another man. But since she won't find Landon, she doesn't need to know that. "Not much of a wedding guy. I'll send you a nice gift though."

She chuckles. "No, you have to be there. You're the beta helping me find my alpha."

The beta. She just called me the sidekick, the one that doesn't get the girl. Anger and jealousy burn in my gut even though this was my idea in the first place. There's a twisted part of me that wants to show her I am the alpha and she's the luna, the female wolf who belongs to an alpha.

An image of her in my bed with her hair spread on my pillow flashes in my mind. Her perfect tits would be pointing up, her chest heaving with every breath. She'd be pleading for her orgasm in that soft, breathy voice. Begging her alpha to let her come.

Fuck, my jeans grow impossibly tighter. At least,

it's dark enough that she can't see the hard-on I'm sporting.

"Your place is pretty." She sighs. "I wonder what his place looks like."

For just a moment, I let myself think about what it'd be like to have her here in my cabin. I have plenty of space in my office. Would she sit at her desk and type away on that old laptop while drinking those overpriced coffees she loves so much? Would her cat play at my feet while I read out another scene? Would I steal kisses from her between chapters?

Shaking my head, I dismiss the stupid fantasy. I've been alone my whole life and that's not about to change.

5
GWEN

Blade leaves the truck as soon as I acknowledge how pretty his place is. *Try to give the guy a compliment.*

He's around my side a second later and opens the door for me. He did it earlier too. He's always opening doors for me. I wonder for a moment if he has a wife or girlfriend and force myself to ignore the stab of jealousy that hits me.

When I try to reach for the cat carrier, Blade takes it instead. He's so thoughtful, always doing things for me. Maybe it's just the way guys in his town behave. I'm not sure. All I know is that I like the way the moonlight glints off his bicep as he easily takes the carrier.

As I approach the cabin, the moon bathes it in a

soft glow that makes the place look magical and inviting.

I love living near the beach and hearing the sound of the ocean hitting the sand. I love the way the air always smells salty, and the way the heat is so oppressive in the summers.

But I can't deny that lately, I've started to feel a bit lonely there. What would it be like to have a little mountain cabin? To watch the sun rise on the porch swing while sipping my coffee? To leave the bedroom windows open at night so I can smell the pine trees and fresh air?

Blade stops on the porch. His voice is gritty when he speaks, "What has you convinced he's the one anyway?"

I don't know how to explain it to Blade. I don't know how to explain it to anyone. I only know that my soulmate is here in Courage County, and I want to find him. I desperately *need* to find him.

Blade has already made it clear that he doesn't understand this, my quest for true love. I don't know why it disappoints me that he doesn't get it. For some crazy reason, I find myself wanting Blade of all people to support me.

I finally settle on shrugging, the strap from my purple bag digging deep into my shoulder. My stomach growls, reminding me that I haven't eaten in hours. I don't normally skip meals, but I was too nervous at the thought of meeting Landon to eat anything after my book signing.

Blade sets the cat carrier down and turns to me. If I thought he was handsome in the light of day, it's nothing compared to how he looks in the moonlight. All harsh lines and deep shadows. He's mysterious and striking and breath-taking in his fierce beauty. "You can tell me."

I shift my weight, and a porch board groans beneath my feet. I went skydiving last year and spent most of the night before so nervous that I thought I'd throw up and so excited that I couldn't sleep. That's exactly how I feel when I'm standing next to Blade. Like I'm about to do another freefall.

An owl hoots in the distance, and the wind rustles through the long grass. Nature is oblivious to our conversation. To the way my heart is pounding, and my blood is buzzing.

What would it be like to live here with him? Would he spend his days watching as I type furiously? Would he bring me a fresh cup of coffee when the writing is going really well? Would he massage my neck when it's tight, and I just need a moment of encouragement and the reminder that he believes in me? And why am I even thinking about these things when it comes to Blade?

"It's complicated," I finally murmur. It's a lie, and we both know it. Complicated is the word people use when they can't face the truth.

Fortunately, Blade doesn't press me about it. He probably just thinks I'm some ditzy romance writer anyway. I don't know why that thought hurts, but it does.

"Do you have a girlfriend or wife?" I ask as I follow him into his cabin. Maybe it would be better if he did. Then my brain could get back to focusing on Landon. I'm not even sure what it is about Blade. Maybe it's just because he's a puzzle and the writer in me needs to understand what makes him tick.

I don't know what I was expecting inside his cabin, but it wasn't this. The hardwood floors are covered in oval rugs in cheerful colors and the furniture has quilts strewn over it. The place looks cozy and inviting, and more than that, it feels like home. I breathe in deep, trying to memorize the smell of pine and his cologne.

Blade grunts his response.

"I'll take that as a no then." It makes me happy to know that Blade is single. I'm usually the one that's excited to hear when people are happily coupled.

But I don't want to know that the sexy mountain man is with anyone else.

Inside, he sets the kitty carrier down again and reaches for the latch. "Do you have food?"

"Of course." I scowl at him. What kind of pet mom does he think I am? I might have skipped lunch, but my boy got a healthy meal. "And he's trained, sort of. Alvin can be...well, he gets into trouble sometimes."

"You named your cat Alvin?" He asks as my gray fluffball scrambles out of the carrier.

"Yes," I explain as Alvin rubs himself against my legs. I lean down to scratch behind his ears. "He's getting a brother. As soon as the shelter says he's healthy enough, I'm bringing Simon home. They've already bonded."

Having a companion might help Alvin mellow some, but I doubt it. Not that I would change my kitty. Alvin is perfect just the way he is. Accepting your baby is what being a pet parent is all about. That's what being any type of parent is about.

I straighten and glance around the cabin that holds no photos, although there is a cool-looking gargoyle made of metal on his side table. I step forward and run my fingers along the intricate artwork, unable to resist touching it. "Do you have any family living nearby?"

Something flashes across his features, a hardness creeping over them. "No family."

"Anywhere?" I prompt. Sure, I can't call my parents if I need them. I'd never tell them if I was short on rent money, and I definitely can't tell them about the trouble with my car. But still, I have the knowledge of where I come from and who I am. Does Blade not have that too?

He turns and strides from the room toward the kitchen. His big boots clomp along the floor as he goes. For a second, I wonder if he's mad at me.

I hurry after him on my short legs and reach for the back of his t-shirt when he stops in front of the fridge. I don't know why I want to touch him, but the moment I realize what I'm trying to do, I drop my hand so I can't make contact. "Sorry. I ask too many questions. I always have. I'm curious about the world around me. Maybe, that's why—"

He spins around so fast that I stop talking and glares at me. His nostrils flare, and there's fire in his gaze. "Don't you ever apologize for being yourself. Not to me. Not to anyone."

I swallow, the sound loud in the small space. Other

than Zoey, I've never had someone that didn't want me to apologize. That didn't ask me to somehow make myself less. Less loud. Less vibrant. Less big.

We live in a world that celebrates women that make themselves small—the selfless ones that give and give and give while never taking for themselves. The ones that lose weight then more weight then more again. Until they're only shadows of who they want to be.

I barely know Blade, and he doesn't mind if I take up space or ask questions or follow him around his cabin. My eyes tear up at his unexpected words, and the way they soothe an ache in me that I didn't even realize was there.

He cups my face in his roughened hand. His thumb sweeps across my cheek gathering up the lone tear. "You deserve better than all the ones that said you had to change."

I manage what I hope is a smile. How is it that this man can see straight into my soul? How can he lay me bare with just one look?

He lowers his head, his lips just inches from mine. We're sharing the same air, our breaths mingling. His lips are so full, so kissable. For a second, I think he's going to kiss me, and my heart pounds in my chest.

But then I think of Landon and how much I like him. Despite the fact that I want this kiss more than anything, I step away from the mountain man. He might be an amazing guy, but he's not my soulmate. "I'm sorry. I can't. Landon—"

"Is a coward that doesn't even have the guts to meet you," Blade spits out.

"My soulmate is not a coward." I'm not even sure how I can go from wanting to kiss Blade to wanting to throttle him all in the same breath. Landon wouldn't be like this. He wouldn't confuse my feelings and frustrate me.

"He's a horse's ass. Any man that isn't willing to put everything on the line for you isn't worthy of you in the first place," he argues.

"He's just shy." That has to be the problem, right? Landon is introverted and cautious. It's not that he doesn't want to meet me or see me or fall in love with me. He's just hiding, and it's my job to draw him out of his shell. "He's an amazing guy. You'll see."

6

BLADE

This woman is driving me crazy in the best way. I want to spend my days kissing her and arguing with her and giving her endless pleasure. If she could just get over this obsession with Landon and soulmates.

"He's just shy," she insists.

I'm not her soulmate. I know that without a doubt. But that doesn't mean we couldn't have some dirty fun together. Hell, something tells me the chemistry between us would be downright explosive.

"He's an amazing guy. You'll see." Except that when she says it, she sounds like she's trying to convince herself. Maybe she has doubts about Landon. Hell, I can help her along with that.

Once I prove to her tomorrow that Landon isn't

coming around for her, I'll take her back here. We'll spend the next two days in my bed where we'll both get what we want. She gets the knowledge that she tried her best to find him, and I get to hold my fantasy woman. At least, until she leaves.

Forcing myself to relax my tensed shoulders, I answer, "Then I look forward to meeting him."

She tilts her chin up. "You'll love him. The two of you will be best buds before the day is up, and you'll be invited to my wedding."

The thought of Gwen in a white dress does something funny to my insides. Makes them hurt in a way they never have before. I rub my hand over my chest and turn to the fridge. "Can't wait."

I pull out the marinated steak and gesture for her to follow me. She gasps as she steps outside onto the back deck. The view is spectacular. That's why I chose to build my cabin here. On clear nights like this one, you can see the other mountains around us for miles while the stars overhead shine like beautiful nightlights.

The back deck is my favorite area and where I spend most of my time when I'm not reading naughty books for Gwen. There's a pavilion over it to provide shade during the heat of the day. A table and chairs give me a comfortable place to relax. The twinkle lights wrapped around the wooden columns keep it lit at night without disturbing the nocturnal wildlife while the glowing lanterns on the table add a nice touch too.

In the corner, there's a dog dish with food and a fluffy cushion. I don't know much about the skinny, mangy mutt that's started sleeping on my back porch. But I won't deny him a few basic comforts.

Sometimes, I look around at my life now, and I shake my head. I can't believe the same kid who used to fight the other boys for enough to eat now owns a home and some land.

I start the gas grill to the soundtrack of the cicadas and the crickets, singing their love songs.

"Wow," Gwen says in a breathy whisper. The sound goes straight to my cock. I want her whispering like that when I'm thrusting inside of her. I want her voice filled with that much awe and wonder, like she can't believe two people could be that good together. "A girl could get used to a view like this."

Could she? Could she fall in love with the view from my back deck? Could she give up her pretty little home by the beach and settle for a mountain cabin with a grumpy one-armed man?

She turns to me and I busy myself with the grill,

so she doesn't realize that I was staring at her like a creeper. *Let me guess. They didn't want you. No shock there, kiddo.*

The social worker's words ring in my ears again, and I force myself to push them back. There's a reason that I was in the boys' home growing up. Didn't matter how many times I got out, I always had to go back.

Gwen opens her mouth as if there's something she wants to say then snaps it closed again, probably thinking better of it.

I hate when she does that. I hate whoever taught her that no one is interested in what she has to say. "Go ahead and spit it out."

She shakes her head. "I have no filter."

"Don't care too much for people with 'em. You can't trust a person who won't say what's on their mind." There's a reason I got passed over for promotions. I wasn't willing to say what people wanted to hear just so I could get a head pat and an "atta boy".

She licks her lips with no idea how sexy I find the simple gesture. For a romance writer, she seems innocent and untouched. The thought has my cock hardening even more. "Well, it's just…I started thinking…you don't have an arm and you don't have a family and it made me worry that maybe you lost them in like some horrible accident and I poked at wounds that I shouldn't have. I told you. I have no filter and—"

"No reason for apologies," I mutter as I flip the steak. "I was a foster kid. Never knew my family. Never adopted. Lost my arm in the service. Any other questions?"

Her gaze softens, filling with sadness. Fuck, I don't want her feeling sorry for me. The last thing I deserve is pity. I've made shit choices my whole life. "How do you like your steak?"

She blinks. "Blade..."

"You look like a medium rare kind of girl."

She finally nods, seeming to accept that there are things I don't want to talk about. "You read me right, sailor."

I frown, and she gestures to my stump. I have an above elbow amputation, but some of the tattoos are still there among the scars.

"The anchor is a dead giveaway."

We're silent for a few more minutes before she smiles at the dog bowls in the corner. "What's your dog's name?"

"I don't have a dog," I answer, thinking of the white and tan Jack Russell Terrier that sniffs around every so often. Don't even know the little guy's name. Poor fella hasn't been loved well.

"So then you just like putting dog food out?" She laughs. It's a soft, tinkling sound that fills my chest with a funny feeling. I want to hear the sound of her laughter every day for the rest of my life. It's not something I'll get, but that doesn't stop me from wanting it.

"There's a stray that wanders through here sometimes." If there's one thing I remember in my life, it's the feeling of being a stray. The stinging knowledge that I didn't belong to anyone. "I leave food out for him."

"You could adopt him," she says.

I can't explain that I'm not the type of guy that does the whole domestic scene. There's a reason I don't have a wife, two kids, and the truck with toddler seats. I'm not family material. Never have been. Never will be.

Instead of focusing on the life that will never be mine, I pull the steak off the grill and plate it. It's large enough for two. I nod to the cabinet by the grill, and she pulls out the dishes. I grab the waters from the mini fridge.

We settle at the table, and she gives me a warm smile. It strikes me then that she's easy to please, so hopeful to be loved. The realization has me feeling like an asshole for not telling her. It's on the tip of my tongue to confess my true identity.

I stick my fork in my steak and stabilize it with my stump, using my other hand to grip the knife and cut my food. I've done this so many times that I don't have to think about it anymore.

"Did you lose it a long time ago?" She asks.

"Three years back," I answer. "Truth is, I forget about only having one arm most days. When it first happened, it was all I could think about. Now it's just a part of my life. I don't register it most of the time, except when I'm trying to do things like open a pickle jar or cut steak."

She nods, and I can sense all the questions she has. People are curious when you're different. It's something I had to come to terms with after I lost my arm. "I don't mind talking about it."

"Do you have a prosthetic? Wouldn't that make things easier?"

"I know guys that have them, but I didn't like it. It just felt bulky and unnatural to me. Kind of depends on the person, I guess."

I watch her take a sip of her water, the way her bright red lips wrap around the bottle has me shifting in my chair. Everything this woman does is arousing as hell to me. I think again about that scene I read for her. The one where the hero took her against his shower wall after she deep throated him. Fuck, that was hot. Does she ever get horny when she writes those scenes? Does she squeeze her little thighs together and shift in her seat? Does her hand wander into her panties while she strokes that pearl between her legs?

She finishes her sip and looks at me. Something about the way her cheeks color has me wondering if she's thinking about me naked the same way I'm thinking about her naked. "Did you lose it in combat?"

"Just an accident. I was the safety officer, training two new recruits on the ship. A cable snapped that wasn't properly secured. At least, that's what they tell me. I don't remember anything about that day," I explain.

The reports say I shoved the recruits out of the way just in time. Figures the one honorable thing I do in my entire life, and I don't even remember it. "I thought that was a bad thing at first. But some of the men I met had such horrific nightmares and panic attacks. Now I see it as a small mercy."

She's looking at me like I'm her personal hero, and it fills me with pride and warmth. I want to pound on my chest. But she wouldn't look at me that way if she knew the full story. If she understood why I ended up in the military or the choices I've made in my life.

I finish the last of my steak and nod to her. "We should go inside. Get an early start tomorrow, so we can find your soulmate."

7
GWEN

I'm in Blade's bed, surrounded by his pine scent. Except he's not here with me. I'm just staring at the wooden beams in the darkness and thinking about the sexy mountain man.

After he shared some of his story at dinner, he took a couple of blankets from the bedroom and made up the couch without a word. I thought he was giving me a place to crash but then he took it, leaving the bed to me. He nodded and told me to sleep well.

I asked about the other bedroom. There's clearly another room across from his. He told me it was his office, and it's undergoing renovations right now. He insisted there's dust everywhere.

When I tried to learn what he does for a living,

he said he works from home and didn't offer any details. I get the feeling he doesn't like it when I pry, so I didn't ask all the questions running through my head.

There are things he hasn't told me. Things that I think maybe he wanted to share. At least, that's the feeling I got over dinner. I don't know why I feel so drawn to Blade. I think it's just that he needs a friend. Yeah, that explains why I find the man so fascinating. It has nothing to do with noticing that his lips are full or that his gruff mood is somehow sexy.

I sent Zoey a quick text before I laid down for bed. It was a smiling selfie with a caption telling her that my stay at Hotel Grump has been a non-stop thrill ride. Alright, maybe I didn't describe it exactly that way. Still, I managed to sound upbeat and happy in my description of the day's events. Now though, I'm left to wonder about my handsome host.

"Why are you such a mystery?" I ask the darkness as Alvin purrs peacefully beside me. He's usually anxious when we're in new places, but not today. He seems to have adapted to Blade's cabin like it's his second home.

"It's important that you don't read into anything," I warn Alvin. "Don't get attached."

When I still can't sleep, I finally reach for my reading tablet. I've been reading mafia romances lately but tonight, I search until I find a book about a hot mountain man.

During the steamy scene when the hero captures the heroine and takes her roughly in the woods outside his cabin, I put my hand in my panties. I close my eyes and imagine a certain mountain man. As I come, I whisper his name.

The orgasm fades as my muscles relax and I fall into a deep sleep filled with filthy dreams. Filthy dreams about a mountain man with dark eyes and an even darker past.

The next morning, I'm awake before Blade. I get ready quickly because I'm eager for this day to be over.

For one breathless moment, I let myself imagine that Landon was lying to me. Maybe he doesn't live in Courage County at all. He could have just said that so I'd never guess where he really lives. Even as I think the thought, my stomach flips. I don't want to betray him. He's my meant to be.

Blade is still sleeping on the couch. I let myself

take a moment to enjoy how fine he looks in those gray sweatpants with no t-shirt on. I can see all the ink that wraps around his skin, and I long to trace it with my tongue.

I shake my head at the strange urge and tiptoe into the kitchen. I find his coffee maker then quietly search the cabinets for his mugs. Just as the old machine starts a sizzling drip, he wanders in.

I love how he looks with his short, messy hair and the way he's sleepily blinking. There's an obvious bulge between his legs, and I can't help wondering if his dreams were as filthy as mine.

"Hi." I smile brightly at him and try to remind myself of my promise to be his friend. He's lonely, and he needs someone to care. "I'm glad you're up. Today is soulmate day."

He grunts and his gaze rakes over me, taking in my outfit. I picked another short skirt today, and it had more to do with the hungry look in Blade's gaze than it does any desire to impress Landon. The t-shirt with the sarcastic quote on it is tight around my breasts while the V-neck shows off a generous amount of cleavage, thanks to help from my favorite push-up bra. Along with my red heels, I'm pretty sure I look downright fuckable.

He turns away from me quickly, tossing over his

shoulder. "I'll be back and dressed in ten. Be ready to leave."

"I thought we were past the bossiness," I mutter to Alvin as I watch Blade's retreating back. The fact that he looks that sexy just rolling out of bed should be a crime. No man should look that good in gray sweatpants.

Fifteen minutes later, we're on the road and headed into Courage County. Alvin is still at Blade's cabin. He's probably planning to get me in trouble later.

"Where are we going to start our search?" I ask and tuck a strand of hair behind my ear. There's so much tension in the truck. Does Blade regret agreeing to help me? Does he wish he'd just left me stranded on the side of the road?

"Sinful Desserts," he grits out. Why does he seem so angry with me this morning? Won't he be glad to be rid of me? He can go back to his quiet life here on the mountain.

"Why there?" A dessert shop seems a strange place to start our search, unless he knows something about Landon that he isn't telling me. I try to remember if Landon mentioned having a sweet tooth.

He doesn't answer, and we spend the rest of the

drive in silence. Did I imagine the chatty guy from last night? The one who opened up to me just a little bit?

When he finally stops the truck in front of a quaint shop with a red and white awning, I smile. This looks like something out of the small-town romance books I read. "It's an ice cream shop."

"It was, but the owners needed to find a way to keep business going year-around, so the place started focusing on desserts," he explains as we leave the truck. We're instantly engulfed in the warmth of the late spring in the south. It's a sticky humidity that will last from now until nightfall.

"And Landon works here?" I ask hopefully. A lot of people working in the book industry work another job. Sometimes, it's a necessity to keep the lights on. Sometimes, creative people just like having other work to do.

He blows out a frustrated breath, and I can feel the tension rolling off of Blade. The man is wound so tightly. "The book club women of Courage are here at this time of day."

"Meaning...?" I'm still having to take two steps for every one of his. When he realizes that, he slows his pace. But not before I'm thinking about his legs and how his thick thighs fill out those blue jeans of his so nicely. I imagine what it would feel like to sit on his lap, to have my thighs pressed over his.

"If you want to let Landon know you're in town, the gossip mill will be the fastest way to get it done."

"Smart thinking," I mutter. What will Blade say when Landon shows up? More importantly, what will I say? Will I ever see Blade again after I meet my soulmate? The thought sends a pang of loneliness through me.

"Also, the honey buns here are the perfect way to start the day," he adds, as if he knows I have a sweet tooth. But Blade can't possibly know that.

"Wait." I reach out and touch his arm, my fingertips brushing against his inky tattoos. I want to trace all of them, to spend hours exploring every single one on his body. "We can still be friends once I meet Landon, right?"

Something flickers across his face, and I get the same feeling I did last night. Like there's something Blade wants to tell me. Whatever it is, he changes his mind. "Just text the guy and tell him you want to meet him. If he's not an idiot, he'll respond."

I can't tell him that I don't have Landon's number or that I'm terrified he'll think I'm a crazy stalker. "Let's try your way first. I don't want to come off as desperate."

This is the part where he should tell me that the ship has already sailed, but Blade doesn't. He doesn't call me a stalker. He doesn't let me know how ridiculous this whole thing has been. Instead, he just nods. "Then let's get breakfast."

8
GWEN

The little dessert shop greets us with a blast of cool air. The inside has a retro feel with the checkerboard flooring and cheerful, red stools lined up along the ice cream counter. Tucked away in a corner booth are five women, animatedly discussing something. From the way their heads are tucked together and the raucous laughter, they're discussing something naughty.

"This is Cadence and her friends," he whispers in my ear, his breath hot against my skin. He puts his hand on my back, the touch electrifying through the thin material of my tank top. "Come on. I'll introduce you."

He guides me to the table, dropping his hand once we're standing in front of the group. "Hey,

Cadence, think your book club has room for one more? This is—"

"Gwen Hughes!" Cadence exclaims and stands up to greet me. She's bubbly and curvy with a huge smile. She points at the booth. "This is Laura and Molly. They're my neighbors on the mountain, and Ivy works here."

"Can I get you a treat?" Ivy asks pushing from the booth and lightly dusting at her pink apron. With her long hair and fair features, she looks like a princess that just escaped from a fairytale book.

"We'll take a couple of honey buns," Blade tells her and follows her to the register. She tries to engage him in conversation, but he just grunts. She doesn't seem to worry too much about it because she's still happily chatting to him.

"And this is Gabby," Cadence finishes, nodding at the last woman at the table.

Gabby gifts me with another one of her blinding smiles, explaining, "We met yesterday. It didn't even click for me when you signed your name. You write those wolf books!"

The girls invite me into the booth and quickly pull me into a discussion on their book of the week while I sneak glances at Blade and Ivy. She tucks a strand of hair behind her ear as she talks and gives him a smile. Is it a flirty one? Is she flirting with him? Why does that thought make acid burn in my gut?

Laura follows the direction of my gaze. The other three are animatedly discussing the sexy scene where the alpha wolf gave his fated mate a firm spanking after they met for the first time.

"She's not interested in him," Laura murmurs quietly. "She's into Hale. He owns the gym next door, but the guy is kind of dense. I don't think he'd ever take the hint."

"Is Blade into her?" My stupid heart is pounding as I ask the question. I want to march up to him right now and kiss him. I want to show every woman here that he's my man. *Except he's not.* The thought makes my stomach hurt.

"I've never seen him with anybody," Laura says.

Watching them, I can't help but wonder if maybe Blade is the reason I'm here. What if my soulmate isn't Landon at all? What if he's just the man that brought me to this grumpy mountain man?

Blade

While the women go back to their book club discussions, I sit several tables away and pretend to answer emails on my phone. Really, I'm listening into their conversation and zeroing in on Gwen's every move.

Cadence, Laura, and Molly are all married to my friends on the mountain. My friends know that I'm a romance book narrator, but I've never mentioned it in front of their women. Unless that came up in casual conversation, the women probably don't know my true identity. If they did, they'd be nothing but supportive. The romance community is incredibly kind and accepting. It's the place where everyone is welcome, regardless of their tastes or kinks.

She laughs at something one of the women says, her tits shaking with the motion. Ever since I saw her this morning, she's taunted me. I know from the way the pink lacy strap keeps peeking out, that she has something sexy on underneath.

When I went to get dressed this morning, I jerked myself off to fantasies of pulling her tank top down and ripping off her bra. I'd expose those juicy tits of hers to my view. Then I'd lick, suck, and nip at them. I'd drive her wild until she was pulling my hair and begging me to give her more.

I'd yank her short skirt up and destroy that thong she's wearing before I'd slide nine inches deep. I'd make her writhe and moan as my thick cock rammed into her tight, wet hole.

Fuck, I can't be thinking about this stuff in public. Shaking my head, I force myself to go back to my emails. But the entire time, I keep listening to their conversation. I'm waiting to see if someone will unmask me.

Will she be hurt if that happens? If she were disappointed, I could deal with that. I've been a disappointment my whole life. But I'd never hurt Gwen, and I'd never let anyone else hurt her either.

Finally, the club starts to disband. Gwen exchanges numbers with several of the women, and I know within a few hours, news of her arrival will be all over town. After all, Courage is a small place and a famous author is almost like having a celebrity here.

Pride swells in my chest for her. I'm proud of Gwen and all she's accomplished. I've followed her career for years, and she's done some amazing things. I only wish I could be by her side for all the amazing things she'll do in the future.

"Where to next?" She asks as I guide her outside. I'm itching to put my hand on her lower back like I did earlier. Hell, I want my hands all over this curvy beauty.

Before I can answer her question, I spot Roman leaving the gym. He jogs over to me and I introduce him to Gwen. He raises his eyebrows at the introduction but says nothing about who she is. He turned his life around after spending a decade in prison, and now he's the proud owner of a construction company.

Gwen's phone beeps at her and she scowls at it. "My phone is dying. Do you have a spare charger?"

The other guys are starting to filter out of the gym, and they're glancing her way. They're looking at what's mine, and I have the overwhelming urge to start gouging out eyes. I need her away from them. I need her tucked safely out of sight, so no one can see my treasure. "It's in my truck. Wait two minutes, and I'll be there."

I watch her getting into the cab, loving the way her legs peek out from under that too tiny skirt. I'm dying to know what's under it, desperate to know what shade her pussy is. That's something for only me to know.

Glancing back at the guys, I stare them down until they all start finding more interesting things to look at than my woman.

Roman clears his throat, a smirk playing at his lips. We both know damn well I was marking her, telling them in no uncertain terms that she's off limits.

Scowling at him, I say, "I saw Gabby yesterday. She mentioned a hostel that she crashes at sometimes. Says it's co-ed, not always safe."

There's something between him and Gabby. Something I can't quite define. All I know is that there's no way that Roman's truck "breaks down" as often as it does. But with an age gap of three decades, I worry he'll never get up the nerve to ask her out.

His jaw tightens, his body language going from relaxed to furious in an instant. "Is that right?"

"Just thought you'd want to know." There's something strange going on, but I don't know enough details. I overheard Trace and Roman talking once. Apparently, Gabby crashes at Roman's place sometimes when he's out of town. At least, I think that's who has been staying in his space without his permission. But why is she doing that and bunking at the hostel?

"Appreciate it, brother." He nods to the truck. "She's your romance author."

"She doesn't know who I am." Discussing Gwen

isn't why I flagged him down, but there's no way to avoid this conversation. "She thinks I'm some Good Samaritan that's helping her find the real narrator."

"What the fuck are you thinking?"

No one else could talk to me that way. But Roman is different. He's the big brother of our group, always looking out for everyone. "She didn't know it was me at first, and now I don't know how to tell her."

"Well, you better figure it out fast, or you'll break her heart."

I push down the irritation I feel at his warning. I won't break her heart. I'll treasure it. I'll make her mine then show her who I really am. She'll be a little shocked at first but glad that she's found me. Then I'll spend the rest of my life making her happy every day. Yeah, that sounds like a pretty good plan to me.

9
GWEN

I check my phone again for the millionth time before letting the truth settle over me. While I've gotten dozens of texts from the women in the naughty book club and a few from some other women in town, Landon hasn't reached out. I thought for sure that he would. *I thought he would want me.*

Still, I got to spend the day with Blade. He took me all over town and introduced me to a lot of people and some really cool businesses. Part of me wants to pack up everything I own and move here. It's probably silly, but this town and the people in it feel like home.

When we returned from our adventures, Alvin had caused chaos. He scratched Blade's leather couch and destroyed his curtains. He played with the tissue in the bathroom, pulling all of it off the roll. He splashed in the toilet bowl too.

I offered to pay for all the damages but Blade just waved it off. For a guy that lives alone with no pets or kids, he seemed pretty relaxed about the whole thing. I would have thought he'd be more upset.

My phone dings again as I sit here on the couch, and my belly flutters. I can't help hoping that this is finally the message from Landon. Maybe he's been trying to work up the nerve to contact me all day. My excitement dies quickly when I see my mom's name on the screen.

There's a part of me that doesn't want to answer. But I'm afraid that if I don't, then she'll worry. At least, I hope she'll worry. That would be a nice change.

"Hey, mom," I answer, noting how soft my tone has gone. I don't know what it is about talking to my parents that makes me feel like a little kid desperate for their approval again.

I still remember their disappointment when in first grade I couldn't read. I was at the bottom of my class, barely able to understand even tiny words. They set me up with a tutor but not before telling me that Hughes are smart, accomplished people.

"You're still making your little videos and telling people you're going to California," she snaps without bothering to greet me.

"They're just podcasts, and yeah, Mom, I'm still going to be on TV." I rub at my temple. I don't want to have this discussion with her again. I know I embarrass my parents. I know they're ashamed to be these amazing, cerebral professors while their daughter writes "those scandalous sex stories".

"You should cancel the TV appearance. Wait until you've lost fifty pounds," Mom says. "The camera adds ten pounds, and I can only tell my friends you have thyroid disease for so long."

I blink at the unexpected moisture behind my eyelids. Normally, I don't let her barbs get to me. But between her call and not hearing from Landon, my heart is feeling raw tonight. "I do have thyroid disease, Mom."

"That's nonsense. My daughter is perfectly healthy. You're just not trying hard enough," she counters. She and my dad don't have an ounce of fat on their bodies.

"I still have tickets for you and Daddy, if you want to come to the taping." I hate the pleading note in my tone, the way I'm begging her to care about me. If she could just show me even a fraction of the fascination she has with her teaching.

She scoffs. "It's bad enough that you write those books of yours, but going on TV to talk about them—"

"Is my choice, and I'm proud of what I do." I sniff as quietly as I can, hoping she doesn't hear me. "I have to go. I'll talk with you later."

Without waiting for her to say goodbye, I end the call and blow out a frustrated breath. Just once, I wish they could support me. I wish they could be at least a little bit proud of me.

"Want to talk about it?"

I look up at Blade. I didn't even hear him come in. My cheeks flush at the thought he heard my conversation. He knows I'm a disappointment to my parents now. "Parents are hard, you know?"

As soon as the words leave my lips, I feel like an idiot. He told me he was in foster care and never knew his family. "I'm sorry. I bet you think I should be grateful, and I am glad to have them."

"You don't have to justify your strained relationship," he says quietly.

I shake my head, not wanting him to think poorly of my parents. "I never went without anything. I always had a roof over my head and food to eat and—"

"That doesn't mean they were good parents," Blade counters and moves across the room. He hesitates for a moment before taking a seat on the couch. He's pressed up against me, his jean-clad thigh next to my bare one. I can feel the heat coming from his body and more than anything, I want to curl up in his lap just like Alvin does mine. "They're supposed to do that stuff. That's the basics right there."

I blink back tears again for the second time tonight. "When I was little, I couldn't read. I was falling behind in classes. There was nothing wrong. I didn't have a learning disorder or anything. It just took a while to click in my head. Longer than the other kids."

He takes my hand, gently stroking my palm with his thumb. The comforting gesture fills me with warmth. "Not easy when you're always behind everyone else."

"My parents were mortified when they found out. My mom told me that…" I swallow hard, embarrassed to admit this. "That there are plenty of kids at orphanages who would be grateful to trade places with me. She threatened to trade me in if…if I couldn't catch up by the end of the year."

Blade slips an arm around my shoulders and pulls me close. "I'm so sorry, sweetheart."

Sweetheart. The simple nickname soothes an ache deep in my heart. I've never been called by a pet name. "I know it's stupid. But there's part of me that always worries that if I displease them too much, then they'll disown me. After I dropped out of college, my mom wouldn't invite me to Christmas that year."

"And your dad?"

"He does whatever my mom wants," I say. "He's more interested in writing papers that his academic peers can admire than he is interacting with his daughter. Even when I'm there, he disappears into his office and doesn't talk with me."

"You deserve better. You deserve people that remind you of how special you are every day, that celebrate your successes and cheer you on in your failures. You deserve parents that are there for you."

I swipe at my face. Since I'm being honest, I might as well put it all out there. "That's why finding Landon was such a big deal to me. I want…someone to love me. I even bought the perfect fuck-me heels to wear for him. I know you probably think that's pathetic."

"I think that Landon is the stupidest bastard in

the world." Blade leans close and then his lips are on mine, soft and sweet. His kiss tastes of pent-up longing and new beginnings.

When I open my lips for him, he sweeps his tongue into my mouth. He teases me with long strokes, almost as if he's savoring this as much as I am. My nipples are pebbling beneath my lacy bra, and I arch toward him. I need to feel his chest against mine. Need to feel all of his solid places.

He lets go of my hand to pull my hair free from my ponytail and threads his fingers through it. He murmurs against my lips, "Love your hair."

I've always thought it was too thick and unmanageable, requiring multiple anti-frizz products and a careful shampoo regimen. But when Blade says he loves it, I feel it's beautiful.

"Do you still want Landon? Is he the only guy for you?"

I pull away from him long enough to suck in oxygen. Nervous energy flows through my veins. There's so much I want to do with this man, and it's time to let go of my fantasy Landon. "I like *you*, Blade."

A soft smile lights up his features. "I like you, too. Now, come here and let me make you feel good tonight."

10
GWEN

At his invitation, I scramble into Blade's lap, putting my hands on his shoulders for balance. I glance at his arm, studying it. I'm not sure how to ask the questions that are swirling in my mind.

Something flickers across his face, the slightest show of insecurity. "Is it disgusting to you?"

I put my hand on his face, feeling his stubble underneath my palm. It's so scratchy and tough, just like my man. "Not for a second, sailor. Just wondering how…well, if there's anything special I need to do for you?"

He swallows. "Touch it."

Slowly, I run my fingertips from his shoulder to his…I'm not sure what to call it. I study his expression as I do, looking for any sign of pain.

He seems to sense my worry because he says softly, "This is my stump. It's what amputees call their residual limb."

I touch the puckered scars lightly. I'm not a surgeon or doctor, but even I recognize that someone skilled stitched my man back together again. "Does it still hurt?"

"It's desensitized now, so only when I bump it on something. Then it hurts like I've hit my funny bone. The only thing that's strange is sometimes, I swear I can still feel my hand moving. Like when I'm driving and think that my fingers are drumming on the steering wheel."

I lean forward and press a soft kiss to his arm. I don't ever want him thinking that it grosses me out or makes me think less of him. In my eyes, he's an amazing guy, and he always will be. "I'm so glad you stopped on the side of the road for me."

He opens his mouth like there's something he wants to say. Maybe he's going to apologize for being gruff or for teasing me about my nonexistent boyfriend. But whatever it is, I don't want to hear it. "All that matters is that me and my sexy mountain man are together now."

He quirks an eyebrow. "You think I'm sexy?"

My cheeks warm at his teasing tone. I would love

to spend my life here in this cabin, writing steamy books and stealing glances at my handsome man. I don't know if that will ever be a possibility, but tonight, I want to believe that it could be.

"It's a good thing, sweetheart. Because I happen to think you're very sexy too."

"Before we go any further, there's something I should probably tell you. I know that I mentioned all the steamy books I write, but I've never done… anything before." I risk a glance at his face, trying to gauge his reaction. I'm not sure how he'll take this news, and I don't want him rejecting me because of it.

Blade's eyes crinkle at the corners, like he's fighting a smile even as his gaze darkens.

"I mean there's really no reason for me to. I have access to the Internet, and there are plenty of dirty movies. Plus, I kind of think it's a really big deal, and I always wanted to wait for someone special."

As soon as I say the words, there's a part of me that wishes I could take them back. I want to shove all the things I'm saying back into my head. It's one of the things that always embarrasses my parents about me, the fact that I don't know when to shut up and keep my thoughts to myself. But now I've gone and done it. Now I've laid all my cards on the table for Blade to read, and I can only hope that he doesn't reject me.

He takes my hand and puts it over his chest. "That's a good thing, sweetheart. Because I've been saving myself for someone special too. And I know that I finally found her."

"Blade..." I call his name as I feel his heart pound underneath my fingertips. I need to have my hands all over this man. I need his hand all over me. I need to feel our connection and know that it goes both ways.

He chuckles, a dark, raspy sound that will haunt all of my erotic dreams for weeks to come. "What do you need, sweetheart? Do you need me to touch this sweet little pussy? Do you need me to rub your clit while I finger fuck you?"

I squeeze my thighs together and try to reposition myself on his lap. But nothing helps relieve the ache. What I need is Blade. "Take me to your bed."

"Are you sure about that?" He puts a hand on my chin so we're looking in each other's eyes. I'm captivated by the intensity I see on his face. He's harsh and unyielding, a man that won't back down from what he wants. "Once I fuck your pussy, I own it."

It sounds exactly like something an alpha wolf

would say, and I can't help the shiver that travels down my spine. "It's yours."

"Good girl," he croons, probably with no idea how the words make me melt inside or how damp he's made my panties.

"There's...just one more thing," I warn him, my cheeks warming. I hate to bring this up because I don't want either of us thinking about another man right now. "I didn't...well, I came here, and I didn't bring condoms."

"Are you on birth control?"

"The pill," I explain.

Disappointment flickers across his features, even though I don't understand why. Blade's life is too quiet and orderly. There's no way he wants to add the chaos of a romance writer and babies. As soon as I think the thought, I see Blade rocking a baby girl to sleep while he sings to his toddler son. The mental image sends a wave of longing through me.

He kisses me again, his tongue tangling with mine until I'm rocking against him and moaning into his mouth. He's so hard, and I grind down. I'm on the edge, only seconds away from coming right here.

"Wait," he breathes out when he finally pulls away from me. His hair is mussed from where I was running my fingers through it. "The first time you come will be on my tongue."

I clench my thighs together. "I don't really need—"

He arches an eyebrow and the look he sends me is molten lava. "Your pussy is mine. I get to decide how you come."

His words make me shudder and more moisture gush into my panties. This man is going to wreck me in the best way. "I need it now."

"Then get naked and get in my bed." He squeezes my ass cheek with his big hand, and it's exactly what I need to hop off his lap. He stands and takes my hand, leading me into his bedroom.

"Strip," he demands the moment we're inside.

I pull off my skirt and tank top quickly. Not only have I never had sex, I've also never shared my body with anyone else. I've never sexted or shown a guy what I look like without clothes and now, I can't help but feel anxious.

Blade reaches for the center of his jeans and cups his manhood. "Damn, you're the stuff of wet dreams. All those beautiful curves on display for your man."

His words help me to relax. He likes what he sees. He more than likes it if the way he's staring at me is any indication.

I bend and reach for the straps of my heels, aware of the way he can see straight down my bra like this. If he likes the view, let him look.

"Bra and panties off. The fuck-me heels stay on," Blade insists, his voice rough. "On the bed. On your back. Pretty thighs spread wide for me. Gonna lick my pussy now."

I peel the last scraps of material from my body, relieved to know he's going to take care of this insistent ache between my thighs. Although if I'm being honest, I could probably come just from hearing him say those dirty words in that voice of his. *The voice that sounds so familiar.*

I push the thought away. I refuse to think of a man that can't even send me a text while I'm here with Blade who's made it obvious he wants me.

Quickly, I get comfortable on the bed. My juices are already dripping from my pussy and if it weren't for the way that Blade's looking at me, I'd find it a little embarrassing. But something tells me that he doesn't see it that way. No, nothing that happens between me and Blade could ever be embarrassing or wrong.

He yanks off his shirt but doesn't remove his pants. Instead, he strides to the top of the bed and reaches for my hair. He spreads it across his pillow before he gives a satisfied nod. "Perfect."

This has to mean something, right? He said he was saving himself for someone special.

Before I can think on that, he's positioning himself between my thighs. He spreads my pussy lips with his fingers and stares at my wetness for so long that I start to squirm. "Want to memorize this moment," he grunts. "It's the last look at my girl's virgin pussy."

Then he dips his head and runs his tongue along my seam.

I jerk at the otherworldly sensation, at how amazing it feels to have his tongue touching such an intimate part of me. But Blade just puts a hand on my stomach, applying the slightest pressure to still me. "Let me eat my dinner, woman."

He growls and grunts as he consumes me, pushing me higher and higher. I try to call out, to warn him that I'm about to come. But he doesn't stop.

"Come for me," he demands, sucking my swollen nub between his lips.

His commands, the noises he's making, the way he's holding me with the slightest pressure, everything about this moment feels sacred and precious.

Then he swirls his tongue around my clit, and I detonate right there. Wave after wave of pleasure pulls me under, and I scream his name in bliss.

When it's over, my taut body relaxes, and he crawls up the mattress to join me. I realize belatedly that he's fully naked now, and that's one show I wish I hadn't missed. He lies down on his side, facing me.

"Hi," I whisper the word, my cheeks warm when I think about where he just was.

His answering grin is wolfish, reminding me of a predator that's spotted prey. "No need to feel shy, sweetheart. Eating your pink little cunt is now my full-time job. I'm going to be doing it day and night."

My pussy spasms in response. I didn't even know it was possible to have a mini orgasm from a guy's filthy words. "If you'll always do that, then I'll have no complaints."

"Damn straight you won't." He reaches for my leg and hooks it over his hips. The position opens me up, and he scoots closer. His cock nudges my slick folds. We both groan at the contact. "You're going to come for me."

"I don't know if I can," I whisper the words even though I'm already on edge again. My breath comes in tiny pants, and my whole skin prickles with the awareness of an impending release.

He brings his hand down and delivers a stinging smack to my pussy. The gesture is so hot, so filthy, and possessive. It sends a flood of moisture pouring from my body as I whimper his name. If he keeps doing things like that, it won't take much more.

He slips his massive cock inside of my wet channel, pausing when he hits my barrier. "This is your last chance to run before the beast consumes you."

I cup his face in my hand. He's saying the dirtiest things, but it's not lost on me that he chose a position that's intimate, that allows me to see his face. For a man like Blade, that's a lot of trust and intimacy. "I want you."

Something flickers across his face, some sadness that he normally hides away from me. It strikes me then that in some ways, Blade is like me. He's never known what it's like to be wanted.

With a savage grunt, he pushes through my virginity. There's the slightest pinch of pain then it's over. All I'm left with is a feeling of fullness and completion, like I found a piece of my heart I didn't know was missing.

Blade stills when he's fully seated inside of me. Sweat beads on his forehead, and his eyes have the glassy look of a man on the edge. "Fuck, I'm addicted already."

I squeeze him tighter, wanting to give him every ounce of pleasure that I can. "Then move, dammit."

He begins a slow rhythm, easing in and out of my body. He plays with my clit each time he pulls out, winding me tighter and tighter.

"Come for me now, my good girl," he whispers just as he pinches the swollen nub.

My pussy flutters around him, strangling his cock as I come in a rush of ecstasy so blinding that the whole world fades. There's only me and Blade and the incredible pleasure he's giving me. I feel the moment his release starts. His hot come fills me, making me send up a prayer that this man can be mine forever. That one day, we can make a baby and have a family together.

11
BLADE

There's nothing like watching my girl in the mornings. She stretches and yawns like a satisfied cat. Then she gives me a sleepy grin that always makes me feel like the luckiest bastard in the world.

We spent the past two days here in my cabin. I don't want her to go. She's mine, and I have to find a way to convince her to stay forever. But for now, I asked her to stay until the taping. It's not much, but it's a start. I still have to find a way to tell her that I'm Landon Shaw.

"What are we doing today?" She asks me, her eyes still glassy from sleep. She sleeps hard whenever she's in my bed. But that could just be because I keep waking her for quickies throughout the night. It's not my fault. It's impossible for me not to touch this beautiful curvy goddess.

"Whatever you want," I answer, as I run my fingertips along her bare shoulder. She's given up on wearing clothes to my bed. Hell, if I had my way, she wouldn't wear clothes at all around my cabin.

"You promised to show me your archery skills." She pouts. I'm powerless to resist her when she gets like this. Actually, I'm powerless to resist her at all. She only has to look at me with those dark eyes and pleading expression, and I'll do whatever she wants. She holds all the power between us, and that should scare me to death. But for some reason, it doesn't. After years of wandering this earth alone, I finally found my purpose. It's to celebrate, champion, and love this incredible woman.

Love? Is that what this funny feeling in my chest is? Is that why the thought of her leaving makes me feel like I can't breathe?

I didn't realize it was possible to care this much about another human being. My goal in life is no longer my own happiness or well-being. It's hers.

"I always keep my promises," I tell her despite the fact that my throat is thick with all the things I want to say. I have to tell her who I really am, but I can't risk her walking away from me. I won't survive that.

"You're going to hit that target?" Gwen asks, doubt coloring her tone. It's not hard to guess why. My target is roughly ten inches in diameter, about the size of a standard DVD.

I think of how round Jacob's eyes would go if he saw this. I texted him earlier this morning, hoping he'd come out with me and Gwen. I think she'd really like him. But Duke called to say that Jacob has a cold.

"Yep."

"From this distance?" Gwen's face scrunches up as she looks between the bow and arrow I'm holding and the target seventy meters away. It's the distance used in the Olympics, and yeah, I'm showing off. Knowing that I'm about to impress my girl sends a thrill through me.

"Better question is what you'll give me if I make it." I love teasing this woman. I love the way her cheeks flush, and she dips her head when I've embarrassed her. "How about another taste of that pussy?"

"Seems like more of a prize for me."

She still doesn't understand just how irresistible I find her. She doesn't know that I need to taste her more than I need my next breath. She's consumed me, body and soul. She's all I think about, the only person on my mind. I'd do anything to go back and change our meeting. I wish that we had started out differently. I wish she knew that I'm Landon. "That's because you don't understand how obsessed I am with your pretty cunt."

"Blade..." She calls my name in part embarrassment and part arousal.

I give her a wink, knowing already that I've made her wet with my crass words. I've never talked this way to a woman in my life, and if it were anyone else, I wouldn't be saying these filthy things. But there's something about Gwen that brings out the primal side in me.

I slip into my gear easily, practice having taught me exactly how to draw the bowstring with my teeth using a mouth tab I made myself. The muscles in my jaw and neck burn from the tension, but I ignore it. The only thing I'm thinking about is impressing Gwen and getting her back to my cabin where we can spend the rest of the day naked.

I release the tab and the arrow flies straight, hitting the target with expert precision. It's a perfect bull's-eye. Normally, that sight alone is enough to fill me with pride. But when Gwen jumps up and down and claps her hands together, a new sense of satisfaction fills me. I did that. I delighted my curvy goddess and made her tits bounce.

"Can you show me how to do that too?" She's looking up at me with those big, brown eyes, and there's nothing I can deny her. She's my whole world now, and she'll never want for anything again as long as she lives. Certainly, not affection or protection or love. She'll have all of those things from me in spades.

I gesture for her to come closer, and when she does, I kiss her with all the longing and love I feel. I can't tell her I love her quite yet, not until I make my confession about Landon. But once I do that, nothing will stop me from claiming Gwen for my very own.

I spend the rest of the morning teaching Gwen how to shoot an arrow. She's not a natural, and she misses almost every shot. But I don't think that's why she wanted me to show her how to shoot. No, if the way she's pressing her ass up against my groin is any indication, she's far more interested in teasing and taunting me than she is learning this sport.

Gabby calls just as were finishing the lesson, and it's the only thing that keeps me from turning Gwen over my knee and warming her bottom for the way she's been teasing me for hours. The thought of her on my lap, squirming and pleading for mercy has my cock even harder.

As we ride in my truck to the auto shop, Gwen fidgets in the seat beside me.

"What's on your mind?" I've never been like this with another person. I never cared what anyone else was thinking, but with Gwen, I find myself wanting to know everything in her head. I want her to share every thought she has with me. I want to know what troubles her, both the big and small. I want to be the man that is always there for her.

"Why do they call you Blade? I mean, it's not like it's a terribly common name. It just seems that maybe it's a nickname, but then where did you get it? Why does a guy that's good with a bow and arrow get called Blade?"

I squeeze my hand on the steering wheel. There are things about myself that I don't want to tell her, but I know if we're going to have a real relationship, then she has to get to know me. The real Blade, the one I don't want her to see. "I got it at the boys' home. I stabbed some of the bigger boys when they wouldn't stop picking on a little runt. We weren't allowed weapons, but I had the ability to turn anything into a blade."

"You must've been put in a rough home." She sounds sad for me. I don't ever want her to be sad, not over me.

"I'm not worth your pity." Acid burns in my gut. She needs to know the type of man I am. She needs to know what I'm capable of. "I ended up in the military because I mugged someone. He was a little old man. I took his cash and his wallet. Then I shot him. Just because I was a selfish prick. I'm not a good man. I never have been, and I won't pretend to be one now."

"Wait, how did you end up in the military?"

"The guy I mugged was a former captain, and he saw I was on the wrong path. He could have used his influence with the judge and the district attorney to send me away for a long time. But instead, he worked out a deal, and as long as I stayed in the military for four years, my record would be wiped clean."

I shake my head in amazement. I still can't believe that he did that for me. The man had every right to hate me. I took his mobility, and he walked with a limp for the rest of his life. But he wouldn't let me throw mine away. He was the only person who gave a damn about me.

"Where is he now? Are you still in touch with him?"

The familiar swell of grief hits me in the chest. "He passed away about two years after I got in. Up until then, he regularly sent me care packages. He made me feel like…I could be more than the cruel bastard I was."

"He changed your life." She smiles at me. "If you had been in prison, your life would've taken a different trajectory. We never would have met. Kind of crazy to think I owe so much to a man I'll never even know."

I think about how I'll never get to introduce him to Gwen or our children. I think about how he'll never get to see me put a ring on her finger. He changed my life forever. Because of him, I'm going to have a family one day.

12

BLADE

"See? That's so much better," I say to the formerly mangy mutt. He shakes himself off again, throwing water droplets on me. But I just laugh it off. After I came home with Gwen to find him skulking around the deck again, I decided enough was enough. The poor guy had matted fur, and there were all sorts of things stuck in it.

I gave him a clipping, as best I could without the right tools. Then I hosed him off and washed him with soap. He peppers me with doggy kisses in thanks, and I can't help laughing at his antics.

I toss a ball with him for a few minutes, surprised how much I like the domestic scene. Gwen is on the deck with her laptop. She's working on her latest book, and part of me wants to know what it's about.

But I'm trying to be patient and let her tell me in her own time.

Still, when I come up behind her, she's not paying me any attention. It gives me a chance to see what's on her screen, and I grin. My girl has a fun side, and I'm going to help her explore it. Right now.

My dick is so hard that it's painful in anticipation of the game we're about to play. Dropping to my knees, I press a gentle kiss to the lobe of her ear. She always has this delicious vanilla taste. I should know. I've spent most of our time together eating out her beautiful pussy.

She startles at my sudden nearness and pulls out her earbud. "You scared me."

"Run." My voice is a deep, dark growl.

She frowns at me and glances at her laptop screen. I see the moment recognition flashes across her face. She's on her feet in an instant, eager for this new adventure of ours. Then she's running through the cool grass, her giggle floating on the breeze.

I pause long enough to close her laptop where she has a webpage open on the benefits of primal play. If my girl wants to play, then I'll play.

My heart thunders in my chest as I chase after my curvy woman. This is what I was made for, to spend my days pursuing this woman who sets my soul on fire. I'll do it all the days of my life, and I'll do it with a smile on my face.

"You'll never catch me," she taunts.

She giggles as she darts through the grass, moving in a zig-zag pattern to avoid getting trapped by me. Well, it's an attempt anyway. I have sheer strength and will on my side. Just as she reaches the edge of the yard, she slows. If she moves further she'll end up in the forest.

I take advantage of her moment of hesitation, slinging my arm around her. I pull her back onto the soft grass with me. Even as we start to fall, I twist so I take the brunt of it. My girl never has to take any blows, not so long as I'm there to absorb the impact.

She tries to struggle against me, but even with one arm, I'm still stronger. It only takes a quick roll and she's underneath me. I use my body weight to pin her down. Before I go any further, I take a second to study her. Her hair is messy and her chest heaves with every breath, pushing those delicious tits against me. But it's her eyes. The wild, feral expression in them makes me feel like a damn king.

She understands what I'm doing—the way I'm checking in with her—and gives me the slightest nod before she sinks her teeth deep into my good shoulder.

I let out a roar and yank on her hair, the motion exposing the creamy skin of her neck to me. Damn, she's beautiful especially when she's like this, savage and unrestrained. I rake my teeth along the column of her throat. "Naughty girl."

She shudders underneath me, arching her hips up and trying desperately to find friction against me. But I'm the one in control here, and it's damn time she remember that.

I flip her onto her stomach easily. She might be considered big by society's standards, but she's no match for the beast she picked a fight with. She's smaller than me, delicate, and I'm going to remind her of that by taking her at a punishing pace.

I keep just enough weight on her to reach for her waist. I flip that cute little skirt up. Once she agrees to be mine forever, that's all she'll get to wear. As her man, I'll demand easy and frequent access to my pussy so I can rut into it day and night.

Yanking down her panties, I grunt into her ear, "I'm going to fuck you like an animal now."

She moans, her cheek resting in the soft grass. The sound is loud in the afternoon as birds flitter overhead and a squirrel moves in the tree above us. Nature is our welcome voyeur, inviting us to lose our inhibitions.

"Put your hands under your chest. Pinch those tits."

She does as I ask but it's not easy. I've pinned her down and she has to work to get her arms free. She gasps as soon as she touches her pert breasts.

"Harder." I swat her ass cheeks, liking how they turn slightly pink. Yeah, I'm definitely going to punish her ass at some point. With the way she gushes more moisture, the idea arouses her as much as it does me.

She gasps as she clutches her tits. Her nipples must be tingling and burning right now, sending bolts of pleasure straight to that perfect pussy of hers.

I yank my cock free from my pants and shove deep into her little pink hole. She's so damn wet, I slip in easily and squeeze her hip. "Thrust your sexy ass up."

She does as I instructed, meeting each of my brutal thrusts. My balls slap against her and she whimpers with every invasion of my thick cock. "You like the way this feels? You like being made to take it deep? To know your man is rutting into you from behind?"

She moans again, the sound as if she's being drugged. Feral satisfaction goes through me at the noise. She's drunk off my cock, off the way it's ramming hard into her tight cunt.

I snap my hips forward. "Answer me."

"Yes!" The word comes out as a startled cry, her release beginning. Her pussy clamps on me so tightly that it's painful but I don't stop. Can't stop. I just keep giving it to her, thrusting deeper and deeper until she collapses with a guttural noise.

Even then, I continue fucking her. Rutting into her like the animal I am, desperately seeking my own release. It's not until I'm shooting my come deep into her pussy where it belongs that my body finally starts to relax.

She hums when I fall into the grass beside her. I pull her onto my chest, needing to feel her against me. I need to be touching her now, seeking reassurance that I didn't hurt her. I'd rather lose my other arm than ever hurt her. "Are you good?"

"Best sex ever." She giggles. "I am so putting that as a scene in my book."

Could I be that guy? The one who stars in the love story of her life? Something squeezes deep in my chest, and I know this is it. This is the moment when I come clean to her. Pushing myself to sit up, I give her a small smile. She'll forgive me for this.

She'll be happy to know who I really am. "Come on, I have something to show you."

I lead Gwen into the house, and she follows me. She's still grinning from our moments together in my backyard. She's flushed and breathing hard. Next time, I'll make sure she's wearing shoes and chase her through the forest. I'll capture her and drag her under a bush and do filthy things to her. Depraved things that will have her blushing for days.

I pause outside my office door and lean over to pluck a leaf from her hair, letting it flutter to the floorboards. "Do you remember when you asked me what I did?"

She nods, her radiant smile still in place. "You said you work from home."

"I do." I open my office door so she can see my space. "As a book narrator."

13
GWEN

My fingers are itching to get to the keyboard as I follow Blade into his home. When I was looking up primal play, I wasn't too sure on the appeal of it. But then he was chasing me through his back yard, and suddenly, I realized it's fun. It's playful and natural and amazing. Now, I can't wait to get back to that scene.

Blade pauses outside the door of his office, the one he said was undergoing renovations. He plucks a leaf from my hair. "Do you remember you asked me what I did?"

"You said you work from home." I can't stop smiling. I don't think I'll ever frown again. Not when I know I have a man as hot as Blade who finds me so irresistible he wants to chase me down and fuck me from behind.

"I do…as a book narrator." He opens the door to his office.

I step into the space and glance around. It's a pretty standard office other than the huge boom mic above his computer. "It's so weird that two book narrators would live in such a small town and not even…"

I stop as I realize what this means. There aren't two book narrators living in Courage County. There's only one.

Landon Shaw.

Blade is Landon Shaw.

I struggle to pull in my next breath as tears fill my eyes. No, it can't be. I'm not understanding this right. I want someone to tell me I have this all wrong. But as I glance at Blade's face, something flickers over it. Guilt.

All those times when I couldn't decide how he was looking at me.

It was guilt.

"You've lied to me." Something pinches in my chest. Is that what it feels like to have a heart attack? I'm pretty sure this sensation that the world is imploding is exactly what it feels like.

"I..." He opens his mouth then snaps it closed. He did lie to me, and there's no defense for that. He knows it, and I know it.

Tears prick behind my eyelids, but I refuse to let them fall.

He makes a pained noise when he sees them, as if it's hurting him to know I'm in pain. But that can't be right. That just has to be my wishful thinking. I've spent so long waiting to be loved that I was willing to accept scraps of affection. Dammit, I really am pathetic. "Did your book club have a good laugh at me? Your friends too?"

"What? No—" He tries to take a step toward me, to do what I don't know.

But I step back. I can't stand the idea that he would touch me now. "It's time for me to go."

"No, I'm not letting you." He shakes his head. "We can talk about this. Yeah, I didn't admit who I was, and that was—"

"Wrong and cowardly," I answer and duck by him. I slip out the door of the office easily. He must have been laughing too. They all must have thought it was funny. *Look at the pitiful little romance writer who just wants to be loved.*

He grabs my arm as I step into the hall. He could overpower me. He could keep me here. Zoey is the only one who knows where I am. But I know instinctively that Blade won't do that. He's a good man, even if he doesn't think so.

I push back the thought. "I gave you my virginity. I trusted you with my body. I gave you everything, and you lied to me."

"And you have every right to be mad as hell about it. But don't walk away from this, from us. You're mine. You're my meant to be."

"Yeah, I thought you were my soulmate. Turns out, I was wrong." I swipe at my face and manage to hold it together. "And you have no idea how disappointed I am."

Blade drops my arm and staggers back as if he's been hit.

I can't believe I did this. I can't believe I fell in love with a mountain man and thought I'd found my forever. I really am naïve.

I move to the bedroom and gather my things. It takes me a few minutes because I've strewn my stuff everywhere. It's all mixed in with his, like I was planning on staying forever. Like I was living some damn fairytale.

Blade watches me the entire time, but he doesn't try to convince me to stay anymore. He doesn't say anything at all.

I help Alvin into the kitty carrier. He makes a mournful noise as he climbs inside, as if he understands that we're never coming back again. This is the last time we'll ever see this cabin. I glance around it a final time, my gaze landing on Blade. His shoulders have slumped and his head is down. Part of me wants to go to him, to comfort him.

But I fight back against the urge. He's not interested in forever. He would have told me his real identity sooner if he'd wanted me. No, it's better if I just leave.

Blade

Waking up on my couch, I stumble toward the bathroom. I reach for the door and scowl when the knob is locked. I jiggle it at the same time a deep voice asks, "What the fuck are you doing?"

I turn and spot Roman.

"Can't a guy take a piss?" My voice comes out belligerent and slow. My whole brain feels muddy, and my mouth is dry as cotton. Fuck, what did I do last night?

"Not when he's trying to piss on my front porch.

Bathroom is that way." He points down his hallway. That's when I realize I'm not in my house at all. I'm at Roman's place.

I move to the bathroom and take care of my business before I splash cold water on my face. I press a hand to my forehead as the events of last night come back to me in pieces. When I stumble into Roman's living room, he passes me a cup of coffee and pain relievers.

"Are you ready now to tell me why you showed up at my house at midnight screaming like a banshee, drunk off your ass?"

I try to remember if I actually did that as I swallow the pills. Fuck, I think I did. I think I was an asshole to him. "She found out. She left. You were right. You happy?"

"Fuck, you cared about her. I saw it on your face, and I knew it'd be a problem." He moves to the stove to make scrambled eggs. He swears when he drops two of the eggs with his swollen hands. The steroid shots don't work very well for him, and I hate that he's in pain.

Of course, he knew it'd be a problem. Roman is the one that reads all the guys. Maybe it was prison that made him good at reading people. "You didn't hear me. She left. I'm a disappointment. I'm always a disappointment."

He stops cleaning up the messy eggs on the floor and raises to his full height. His voice is tinged with anger. Big brother bear wants to defend me. "She called you a disappointment?"

I down the hot coffee that burns like acid and set my mug on the counter. "Doesn't matter. I disappointed her. Rain check on the eggs for me."

He stops me before I can leave the kitchen, stepping into my path. "No, what did she say?"

"She said she was disappointed." I swallow hard, not looking him in the eye. Why should I be surprised that my soulmate traveled hours to find me only to be disappointed by the guy she met? I'm no one's first choice. Hell, I'm barely last choice. I'm just leftovers.

"She's disappointed that you lied to her, Blade. She's not disappointed by *you*. Do you have any idea how happy that woman looked when she was standing next to you? You'd think she won the fucking lottery her smile was so bright."

Is that true? I think back over the last few days, over the smiles she gave me and the way she let me into her body. She held nothing back from me. The woman who was so scared of her parents' rejection, who wanted nothing more than to be loved, showed more bravery than me. She showed up as her authentic self, and I was a coward. Just like she said.

"I need her in my life," I say, the words settling over me. I know what I have to do. I have to get Gwen to give me another chance. I have to convince her that I want to be the hero in the love story of her life.

14
GWEN

"There's not enough eye cream in the world," I tell Zoey miserably. She's here with me in Los Angeles for the taping of the segment. In an hour, a limo will be arriving to take me to the studio's set so I can film my segment. I'll show up looking like a zombie, thanks to a dark-haired mountain man whose name I won't even speak.

Alvin meows from his place in my lap. He hasn't left my side since I walked out of Blade's cabin. Somehow, my kitty knows I need all the support I can get right now.

The shelter called early this morning. Simon had the last of his shots, and he received a clean bill of health. He's ready to come home when I can get back to Charleston.

"Try this one," Piper says. She's Zoey's sister-in-law, and she's a romance writer too. Even though I've never met her before, Zoey brought her along. I'm glad she did. Piper is sweet and so supportive, just like Zoey.

"Maybe he'll pull his head out of his ass," Zoey suggests. She doesn't know the whole story. I didn't tell her. All she knows is that I fell in love with a mountain man and broke up with him in the space of a few days.

"Gray did," Piper offers. She married her own mountain man after he saved her from a bear when she was on vacation. They had a whirlwind romance, and now they're happily married with a baby. Just like Zoey. They're both so lucky.

"Nothing is going to fix this," I tell them. Blade didn't just lie to me. He let me go. He stood there and said nothing as I walked out the door. After everything we shared, I thought I meant something to him. I thought I was at least worth fighting for.

My phone dings with a notification. The limo is here, and the world expects the bubbly romance writer to show up with her usual enthusiasm. My fans will get nothing less than that. They're why I'm here, and I'll do them proud as I take the stage and represent curvy women everywhere.

The limo ride passes in a blur, so do the backstage activities. I'm vaguely aware that I'm signing autographs for some of the crew members and chatting with them. But it's like I'm watching from outside my body. I don't even recognize the girl that's smiling and laughing along with everyone.

Finally, I'm led to the green room where I meet with Maddy. She's every bit as nice and bubbly as she seems on TV. She greets me with a warm, motherly hug before she hugs Zoey and Piper too. She asks me a few questions and tells me she wants to do lunch after the taping.

"She seems genuine," Piper remarks as she flops down on the couch beside me when Maddy has left.

"A sweetheart," Zoey agrees, sitting on my other side. She puts an arm around my shoulders. "We're proud of you. I hope you know that."

I smile at her words, my first genuine smile since I left Blade's cabin. "I'm proud of me too."

Maybe that's the key. Maybe it's time to stop searching for love and instead, choose to love myself and to embrace my friends that love me.

There's a knock on the door and for a moment, I expect it to be another crew member. They've offered me waters and snacks since the moment I walked in the door. A few have asked for selfies, and

I didn't say no to a single request. I'm grateful to be here today, even if my heart hurts.

But when the door opens, it's not a crew member. It's my mom and behind her, my dad. I blink for a second, certain that I've imagined them here. *Oh, shit, are they here to disown me?* Making a dramatic scene really isn't my mom's style, but there's a first time for everything.

She glances at me sheepishly, looking uncertain for the first time I can ever remember. "Is it OK? Can we come back here?"

"If you can be supportive, sure," I answer, keeping my voice casual. I remind myself again about my determination to love myself. I'm done asking for scraps from my parents. I deserve real, authentic love in every relationship.

"I want to grab one of those delicious looking Danish pastries," Piper announces and Zoey follows her from the room.

My mom fidgets with the collar of her button-up shirt when it's just the three of us. She always looks so professional and put-together. She casts a panicked look at my dad. "This is a bad idea. We should go."

He takes her hands from her collar and gives them a gentle squeeze. He nods his head, as if reassuring her she can do this. My mom is normally so confident. I've seen her give lectures to thousands of students, all eager to hear from her. But right now, she looks sad and awkward. "I'm sorry," she blurts out.

I blink, not sure what she's apologizing for. I've never heard my mom apologize. She's right even when she's wrong. "For what?"

She looks at my dad, her brown eyes seeking his approval. "I said it."

For the first time in my life, I realize I'm not the only one he's ignored all this time. He's also ignored my mom. Part of me wonders if that's why she's always pushing herself to be more, to do more. Is it possible she's spent her life hoping for his affection as much as I've spent it hoping for theirs?

He nods his encouragement. He's engaging with my mom, interacting with her. *What kind of weird day is this?*

"We don't want to lose you," Dad says, clearing his throat. He's focusing his attention on the abstract art painting above my head instead of me.

Mom continues, "We haven't been...supportive or...kind. I've let you think that I was ashamed of you...when the truth is, you're an incredible writer. I read two of your books on the plane. They were good. Really good."

I blink away tears, not wanting to ruin the makeup that's been carefully applied. It's not that my mom thinks my books are good. She's read them. She's paying attention to me. "You said they're scandalous sex stories."

"Maybe…I was a little bit wrong." She flitters about, moving to stand near the couch. She looks lost and sad. That's why I pat the seat beside me.

"I've never felt like I was good enough for you," I admit. It's time to put this all on the table, to have a real conversation with her.

She takes the seat and her shoulders hunch. She looks for a moment as if she's bracing for some kind of blow, but she doesn't interrupt me.

"You threatened to send me away, to replace me with a kid from the adoption agency every time I did something that displeased you." Telling her this is freeing in a way, but it's also making me feel raw and exposed.

Her mouth opens and closes with no sound. For a long moment, I think she's going to deny it. But then, she finally speaks. Unshed tears glisten in her gaze. "I didn't realize…it's what your grandmother used to say to me."

I sense there's more, something she's trying to find a way to put into words.

"I wasn't her real daughter even though I was raised in her house. I was the product of an affair your grandfather had. She was always threatening to send me to the orphanage. She'd spend hours picking me apart. My hair was too thin and my nose was too crooked. I was too bookish, used words that were too smart. Sorry, it's not about me."

She clasps her hands together again. Suddenly, I see her for who she is. A woman that's been just as starved for affection as me. She's been trying to earn it the same way I have, hopeful that with each new accomplishment, someone would notice. Someone would finally tell her that she's good enough to be loved.

I reach out and put a hand on her shoulder. Her mistakes from the past aren't magically better. There will always be pockets of hurt in my heart from where she didn't love me the way a mother should. But something about hearing this has changed the way I see her. She's no longer the villain in my story. Now, she's just another character, a deeply flawed one that's aching to be accepted anyway. "It's OK, Mom."

She shakes her head and tears roll down her

cheeks. "It's not OK. I never meant to carry on the tradition. I was just relating to you the only way I knew how."

"We've both been shit parents," my dad says, coming to take a seat on my other side.

I frown at his use of an expletive. In twenty-one years, I don't think I've ever heard him swear. He's always been so polished, like he was expecting to be called on for an emergency lecture at any moment.

"I've ignored you and your mom, given my attention to other things. Less important things," he sighs and pulls his glasses from his face. He cleans them with the sleeve of his dress shirt, the way I've seen him do a thousand times. "We're here to ask for another chance. We want to do better."

Their words ease part of the ache deep in my chest. We can't go back and change the past, not any of us. But we can move forward together. "I'd like that."

A crew member knocks before sticking his head inside the room. "If you'll follow me, Ms. Hughes…"

"I'm so nervous," I tell them as I stand. I tug my top straight and try to remember that this isn't a big deal. I'm only going to be on national TV with my face splashed across countless social media channels soon.

"You can do this, honey," mom says.

"Go get 'em, tiger," Dad says a little too enthusiastically.

I give them both a smile. Even though it feels weird to have their encouragement, it's still nice. That's when I frown. They were set against doing this only days ago. "Why are you here now? How did you know when the taping would be?"

"Landon came to see us," Mom explains.

My shattered heart skips a beat. I open my mouth to ask more questions when the crew member says, "We really have to go, Ms. Hughes. You're on in sixty seconds."

15
GWEN

My face feels frozen in a permanent smile. I've answered so many questions for Maddy and the audience members. Everyone has been amazing and kind, but I can't help wondering about Blade. Why did he talk to my parents? What does it mean that he sought them out? Does this show he cares about me?

The thought makes my stomach flip. Should I call him? Will he call me? Maybe it was just his attempt to fix what happened between us, and it doesn't mean anything at all. Ugh, I need to have a discussion with Zoey and Piper. They'll know what it means.

"And before we go, we have a very special guest here to share how your books have changed his life." Maddy beams at me, interrupting my thoughts about the man I can't seem to get out of my head. "Are you ready to meet him?"

I give her an enthusiastic nod. All I want is for this interview to be over, so I can go and analyze Blade with my friends. Still, this is a fan, and I'll always make time for my fans.

The audience erupts into applause as a broad-shouldered man steps onto the stage and walks toward me. My breath catches in my throat. Blade is here. He's really here with me on stage.

Maddy greets him warmly with a hug and a kiss on the cheek. The woman is happily married to her own supermodel husband with three adorable children and a Yorkie that follows them around. But I still fight the urge to glare daggers at the woman for putting her hands on Blade. I know it's crazy. I don't own the man. But I want to. I really, really want to.

He sits beside me on the leather sofa and takes my hand in his.

"Do you really want to do this?" I ask in a hiss whisper. I don't have a clue what he's about to say, and that makes me nervous.

"Trust me," Blade says so softly that his microphone doesn't pick it up.

I bite the inside of my cheek to keep from telling him that I did that once already. Besides, I want to hear him out. I want to know what was so important that he flew across the country and joined me on TV, after spending so long isolated in his cabin.

"So, Blade, tell us how you first discovered Gwen's books." Maddy is looking at me with a sparkle in her eye, like she has a secret she wants to tell me but can't.

"I was in the hospital after having lost my arm in the line of duty. There was an organization that donated secondhand reading tablets to soldiers. My tablet hadn't been cleaned off, and the previous owner was a huge Gwen fan. I picked up the tablet and began reading one of her books when I couldn't sleep one night."

I swallow against the lump in my throat. "You never told me this." My voice is quiet, meant for his ears only.

"I've never been as brave as you." His lips are only an inch from the shell of my ear, and his breath warms my skin. It reminds me of how he took me bare after chasing me through the grass. A shiver works its way down my spine at the memory. *Was it only two days ago that happened?*

"How many wolf shifter romances had you read before that?" Maddy asks, leaning forward in her seat. The whole audience is listening to us with rapt attention.

Blade's lips are so close to my skin that I feel his smile. I reach out and put a hand on his thigh because I can't be not touching him right now. I can't be not touching him when he's surrounded by all of these women that are looking at him with hero worship.

"None." He lets out a small laugh. The sound is rich and throaty, sending a tingle between my thighs.

"But you were enthralled with her work," Maddy says. It's not a question. It's a statement, like the two of them have already talked about this once before. How could that be possible? How could Blade even get on the show that quickly?

"I devoured every book she's written within a month. I started following her on social media and watching all of her live videos. I became obsessed."

There's the cutest pink tinge to his cheeks under his beard. Blade had a crush on me. I think, maybe he still does. I rub my thumb in a circle on his thigh, fighting the urge to move my hand higher. It would make for some interesting TV if I mauled Blade right here in front of the studio audience.

He continues, "When I saw she was looking for a

narrator, I emailed her and convinced her to give me a chance."

"But you had no experience," Maddy clarifies.

I frown. He didn't tell me that at the time. I'm glad he didn't. It could have changed my decision, and I would have missed out on meeting such an amazing man.

"No experience at all. I learned on the job and well, it turned out pretty great because it gave me a chance to get closer to Gwen."

"And then you, Gwen, traveled to Courage County where Blade lives recently, didn't you?" Maddy asks.

I'm not sure where this interview is headed or what I'm supposed to say, so I just nod along. Are they working together? Is it something they planned, or is this just how the interview is unfolding?

"She was looking for me. I'd accidentally let it slip in a message where I lived, but I never expected her to show up."

"And when she did?"

"I fell even more in love with her."

I freeze as the realization of what he's saying hits me full force. He's in love with me. He's been in love with me, even before I showed up in his town.

The audience members sigh as if this is the most

romantic thing they've ever heard and well, I can't disagree with them. Blade is pretty amazing.

He continues on without Maddy's prompting, "But I messed up. I didn't tell her who I was from the beginning, and I shattered her heart. When she found out, she left me."

"But you're here today," I say softly. The microphone catches my words, echoing them to the audience.

"Yeah, I am, and..." He pauses to drop my hand and dig in the pocket of his jeans. "I have a question for you, Gwen."

Blood pounds in my ears as the audience erupts into shrieks and cheers. "You're kidding me," I murmur in a daze. My hot mountain man isn't really proposing to me. He can't be. This all has to be a weird dream, and I'm still back at the hotel.

He scoots from the couch onto his knees and opens the ring box. He holds it out to me. "Gwen Hughes, I love you. You're funny and fierce and so damn brave. You make me want to be a better man, one who is worthy of you. Will you be the luna to this alpha?"

I throw my arms around his neck. "Yes, yes, yes. I love you too."

Then his lips are on mine, and he's kissing me

with all of the pent-up longing and passion that we haven't shared the last two days.

I tighten my hold on his shoulders urging him even closer and seaming my body to his. I lose track of where we are and who is watching until Maddy's voice breaks through the haze of my lust, "Hey, kids, we have to keep this show PG-13."

I finally pull away from the kiss, which inspires a snarl from Blade. I think he'd keep kissing me forever if I let him…and I don't think I'd mind too much. My mountain man is perfect for me. I can't wait to spend our lives together, learning everything about each other and making love all the time.

"Zoey already has your wedding dress ready for you," Blade's words are soft, spoken for my ears only.

"Zoey and Piper were in on this?" They both played their part so well. Neither of them let me know that they had any contact with Blade.

He nods and gives me a grin that's not even a little bit repentant. "They love me. Their husbands not so much."

I laugh at his words. I doubt that Brock and Gray have any affection for this man. Like Blade, they're very possessive and would hate the thought of their wives talking to another man. "So, you want to get married right now? Were you serious about that?"

He tucks a strand of hair behind my ear, his eyes glittering with love and affection. "I can't wait to spend the rest of our lives together. I already have the chapel booked in Vegas. What do you say?"

"I say I can't wait to be Mrs. Shaw."

"Good girl," he croons, reminding me of all the sexy things we've done together. I can't wait to spend the rest of our lives together discovering all the things that turn each other on.

I turn to Maddy and smile at her, "I'm sorry to go, but I have a wedding to get to!"

16
BLADE

"Blade, we can't do this here!" Gwen moans as I press her up against the elevator wall. I've spent the last two hours on a private plane, thanks to connections from Roman and Brennon. My friends might be reclusive mountain men, but they still wield considerable power in the business world and have access to plenty of resources.

Gwen's friends and family were all around us, drinking champagne and toasting our whirlwind nuptials. I'm not complaining. I'm grateful she has all these people that want to celebrate with her. But it makes it damn hard to fuck your future wife when she's surrounded by her loved ones.

Our taxi arrived at the hotel first, which means

the wedding party won't be far behind us. "Give me three minutes to take you to heaven."

I suck on that spot on her neck that she likes so much. Just like I knew she would, she digs her nails into my shoulders. I wish I weren't wearing this damn shirt, wish I could feel the sting against my skin.

I have no regrets about waiting for this woman. I'll only ever know what it means to be intimate with her. Another woman will never know my body the way she will. I'm only Gwen's, just like she's only mine.

The elevator doors ding open, and I force myself to step back to admire my handiwork. She's heaving beneath that tiny little sundress, her nipples sharp points through the thin cotton. Her hair is mussed from where I've been playing with it and those perfect lips are swollen from my kisses. But it's the beard burn on her neck that I like. It tells the world she belongs to me.

She grabs her hot pink suitcase and rolls it behind herself while I put my arm around her shoulders. I pepper the side of her face, temple, and ear with little kisses as we walk. I can't help it. I need my woman more than I need to breathe.

The moment we're in the hotel room, I don't

even give her the chance to look around. This might be the honeymoon suite, but there will be plenty of time to explore it later. Right now, I have to get to my girl's pussy.

I push Gwen against the door and drop to my knees. I yank up the skirt of her pretty dress, desperate for this. "I've been dying for a taste all afternoon."

I swipe my tongue through her hot, swollen folds. Her vanilla flavor explodes in my mouth, setting off the beast inside of me. My cock hardens to the point of pain and my balls ache. But all that matters in this moment is taking care of her. She's my whole world.

"Blade," she gasps my name and tugs on my hair as I work my tongue into that tight entrance of hers. Her juices are spilling down my face and chin, but I don't care. I want to always smell like my girl's pussy. It's a scent I'll wear with pride.

I work her clit with my thumb, desperate for her release. It's more than just knowing that I can make her come. It's about being the man that meets all of her needs, in and out of the bedroom.

She groans and shoves my head between her thighs, working me right where she needs me. Then she's crying out my name into the room, telling everyone on this floor—hell, probably the whole damn hotel—exactly who's making her come.

When she finally floats back to earth, I pull her skirt down and give her a grin. Watching and hearing her come will always be one of my favorite things.

She reaches for me, cupping my steel rod through my slacks. "You promised me three minutes which means we still have more time, Mr. Shaw."

We won't have long before everyone has caught up to us, but I can't resist the siren call of my future wife. I may have just satisfied her, but she's a greedy little thing. She'll take every orgasm my body will give her, and I'm more than happy to provide them.

"Naked. On the bed. All fours," I grit out while reaching behind her to lock the door. If the rest of the wedding party does make an appearance, I don't want them walking in on her. No one gets to see Gwen's beautiful body but me. I'm the only one who is allowed to worship at the altar of her curves. The only one who's allowed to see, lick, and kiss every inch.

She's taking too long to move so I bring my hand down on the curve of her ass in a stinging swat. My voice is deep, my desire evident as I issue the command, "Obey. Now."

She squeezes her thighs together, and I file away the knowledge that she likes it when I dominate her. We'll have fun with that one later. For now, I need her too badly. As it is, I have to plunge my hands in my pants and squeeze my cock to keep from coming on the spot.

In the time it took me to get undressed, she's already in position on the bed. She's completely bared to my view, all of her soaking holes visible to me. Fuck, she's beautiful like this. Especially when she glances over her shoulder and gives me a mischievous smile, "I obeyed."

I prowl across the room and touch her ass. There's a slight pink tinge where I delivered that smack. Maybe one day I'll paddle her, make her plead with me for mercy then stuff her full of my cock.

"Such a good girl," I croon as I glide into her sopping wet pussy. She's so damn tight for me, always making me work for every inch.

She lets out a keening cry for more, desperate for her man to fill her completely.

"Turn your head to the left," I instruct when I catch a glimpse of movement. The left side of the room is a mirrored wall. "Watch as your man fucks you."

She turns just as I ram deep, stretching her wide for her man. I still for a moment, sweat beading down my back and adrenaline making my hands shake. "You remember this moment. Remember who gets to fuck you every day."

"You do!" She moans as I withdraw.

"Damn straight," I grunt. My balls slap against her as I thrust back inside her sweet cunt. I'm going to spend the rest of my days filling every one of her holes with my come. It will always be dripping out of her, reminding her of who owns her body.

She claws at the bedding, desperate for more. But in this position, she can only take what I give her and the knowledge gives me a rush of power. She's at my mercy, forced to accept whatever my body does to her.

"You want to come?" I snap my hips. Her tits bounce with each brutal plunge, and the sight drives me higher. A tingling sensation builds at the base of my spine.

She makes a noise of frustration, barely able to find her words anymore.

I move my hand and circle her clit. It won't be long before I come, but I need her to go first. She comes first in every area, especially when I'm breeding her precious cunt. "Whose pussy is this?"

"Yours," she cries out just as I pinch the swollen nub.

She explodes all over my cock, moisture gushing from her body and coating me. Fuckin' love the sight of her come on me, of knowing I drove her that crazy. The orgasm that I've been fighting finally pulls me under, the pleasure stealing my breath away.

I flop on the bed next to her completely spent and pull her into my arms. I nuzzle her hair as I listen to her harsh breathing that matches my own. "I love you."

"I love you, my alpha." She giggles at the word then glances at me. A frown creases her beautiful face. "There's so much we haven't talked about. Like, where are we going to live?"

I smooth the frown with my thumb. "You're my whole world. We'll live wherever you want."

"I've always been a beach girl, but the mountains grew on me. I could imagine settling there, writing my books, having kids…" Her voice trails off.

I already know she's worried she said too much. "Never imagined myself being a dad, but that's changed. Since meeting you, I keep thinking about seeing you grow round with my babies. I want daughters with their mother's eyes."

Her smile lights up her face. "I can't wait to build a family with you."

I press another kiss to her lips and my cock immediately hardens again. Dammit, I'm insatiable when it comes to this woman. I'm just about to suggest another quickie when there's a knock on our hotel room door.

She springs away from me. "Send them away. I need a shower. I'm not getting married smelling like sweat and sex."

I sniff her hair. "You smell pretty good to me."

She shoves at my shoulder. "Go take care of them. I'll meet you in there."

17
BLADE

Three hours and one shower quickie later, I find myself in the back room of the chapel. The whole second floor of the hotel is a wedding chapel, complete with dressing areas for the happy couple.

I adjust the bowtie for Alvin. He keeps swatting it sideways. His brother, Simon, is much more relaxed about the little vest he's wearing. I picked Simon up on my way to California. I couldn't go and demand my girl marry me without all of our family being included, especially our four-legged babies.

"Hold still, Theo," Rafe grumps. He's trying to wrestle my little mangy mutt into a doggie tuxedo along with Roman. Yeah, I figured his days of wandering my back yard as a stray are done. He's now proudly wearing a purple collar with his name on it, although the tuxedo is still a work-in-progress. Between Roman's swollen hands and Rafe's twisted arm thanks to cerebral palsy, it's taking both of them working together.

"That's Theodore," I correct my friends. He's already bonding with Alvin and Simon, and I think the three of them will be buddies soon.

Roman rolls his eyes and mutters something about me being whipped.

I ignore the comment, too excited about the possibility of marrying my girl today to care what anyone else thinks. As far as I'm concerned, this is the best day of my life. I'm getting to start my family with the most beautiful woman on earth.

Rafe's phone rings and he pulls it out of his pocket to scowl at it again.

"Is that the fake princess?" Roman asks.

Some scammer keeps calling Rafe and insisting she's a princess and needs to urgently speak to him. Not that he ever returns her messages.

He rolls his eyes and mutes the call.

"Block her number," I tell him.

He smirks. "You've never heard her voice."

I get it then. He likes the sound, that's why he keeps letting her leave messages even though she's obviously trying to run a con on him. Hell, it wouldn't surprise me if he calls her back one day and lets her play the game just so he can listen to her speak.

"Done!" Roman pronounces and leans back on his haunches. He's panting like he's run a marathon but Theodore is now in his snazzy tuxedo. I've always thought dressing up animals for events was stupid, but I know it'll make Gwen smile. That's all the matters to me anymore, finding ways to make my woman happy.

There's a knock on the door, and I call out. I expect to see Gwen's parents. After I sobered up, the first thing I did was go to the fancy college where they teach and demand to see both of them. I made it clear that I'm the man that loves their daughter and if they didn't shape up, they wouldn't be seeing her or any future grandchildren. They were on the plane within two hours of my lecture.

But it's not Gwen's parents. It's the bride herself. She gives me a dazzling smile. She's wearing a white dress with over the shoulder sleeves and a tight, fitted bodice. The puffy, tulle skirt has me longing to stick my head underneath it to find the exact shade of underwear she's wearing. *Is she wearing underwear?*

Fuck, I definitely shouldn't be thinking about that right now.

"You're not supposed to see the—" Rafe starts.

I hold up my hand to stop him. No one reprimands my queen. No one dares to speak to her with anything less than complete respect and adoration. All she has to do is look at me, and I will lay siege to cities. All she has to do is whisper my name, and I will lay the world at her feet. She's my everything.

Gwen gives me a soft smile, taking in the animals. "You made them all look so cute! The girls are going to flip!"

I don't care about impressing her friends. There's only one woman whose smiles I want to earn every day.

"We're going to go check on..." Roman says. I don't even pay attention to how he finishes that sentence. All of my attention is focused on how sweet Gwen looks standing there. Like something out of a dream or a fairytale.

My friends exit the room, leaving the two of us alone.

I cross the floor to take her hand in mine. There's something troubling her, and I want to know what it is. I don't want this day to be anything less than perfect for her. "What do you need, sweetheart?"

"This is beautiful and amazing and so perfect..."

"But?" I prompt. Normally, there'd be a rock in

my gut and I'd be expecting her to leave me. But it's not there today because I'm confident that she loves me just as much as I love her. We can overcome anything together. "You don't want it?"

"It's not that." She shakes her head and puts her hand on my shirt. Even with the layers of fabric between us, her touch warms me. It always will. "I don't want you to feel like you have to make some big, over-the-top gesture. I love you, Blade, just as you are. And I need to know you know that. That you understand how much—"

I stop her words by pressing a gentle kiss to her lips. My heart is too big for my body. It's filled with too much love, and I'll never be able to contain it all. "I want to marry you. I want to watch you walk down the aisle in a white dress. I want to hear you tell your friends and family that you'll be mine forever. And then I want to take you back to our hotel room and make love to you again and again."

She beams up at me. "I like that plan, Mr. Shaw."

I put my arm around her shoulders and kiss her temple. She's so soft and sweet. So mine. "We're going to write a beautiful love story together, and it starts right now."

Together, we make our way to the wedding

chapel. Roman and Rafe corral the fur babies at my feet and take their places beside me.

Jacob is our ring bearer, having recovered from his brief cold. Pride is etched on his little face at being given the most important job. I look at him and hope that one day I get to have sons. Sons to love and mentor throughout their lives.

Gwen's parents walk her down the aisle and pass her to me. They just gave me the most precious treasure in all of the world, and I'll always love her. Always protect and pleasure her.

When the priest pronounces us man and wife, I don't even wait for him to finish. I kiss my girl straight on the mouth, sweeping my tongue into hers. I devour her, like the beast I am because I don't care that we have an audience.

I only let her go when the priest clears his throat and murmurs something about children being present. I break the kiss and pull my wife even closer. I need these curves pressed up against me. Need her to understand that I'm her man now. "You're my fated mate. I'll never let you go now."

Gwen is mine. I've claimed her heart and her soul. I've put my ring on her finger, and there's one last thing to do—put my baby in her belly. I plan to work on that immediately.

EPILOGUE

GWEN

The muscles in my legs are burning, and my breath is coming in short pants. I jump over a branch and pause to listen. Forest noises filter into my awareness. Birds chirp in the trees above me. The wind rustles through the leaves.

A rabbit hops from beneath a bush. I make eye contact with him, and we hear it at the same time. We're two animals of prey being hunted. The heavy thud of my man's boots sets us both in motion. He dives back under the bush while I take off sprinting again.

The past twenty minutes are catching up with me, my body is exhausted from our game. I slow, trying to catch my breath, and he pounces out of nowhere. Like the apex predator he is, Blade cages me into his arms.

His bare chest is hot against my skin, and his heart pounds beneath my ear. But I don't have long to register these sensations before he pulls me onto the forest floor that's muddy from the recent spring rains.

I'm laughing as we go down, delighted to be captured. There's something about running and knowing he's following me. My man won't let me get away, not ever, and something about that makes me warm inside.

He yanks down the top of my dress, exposing my breasts. There's no one out here but the two of us. It's one of my favorite things about living in the country. There are no limits. When we need each other, we just take our pleasure right where we are.

We've been married for a year now, and I expected that we'd stop wanting it so much. But that hasn't happened. It's always so good when we're together, and we're constantly learning more about each other.

"You tried a different trail this time," he growls before he descends on my tits. His teeth scrape against my nipples, and I gasp at the sensation. I've been extra sensitive here lately. I wonder if he's noticed yet.

"Wanted you to work for it," I tease as he bunches up the skirt of my dress. His fingers skim along my belly and don't stop. I can't wait until there's a telltale sign there. For now though, I suppose I should be grateful. I'm not so sure he'll chase me down once he knows.

He runs his hand lower, cupping my wet pussy. He dips a finger inside to find my center already drenched. All I have to do to get like this is put on my special running shoes. Because the moment I do, I know he'll chase me.

Blade lifts his head from my breasts to scowl even as he spreads my moisture around, coating my pussy lips in my juices. "No panties?"

I shake my head, aware that it's messing up my cute braid. I don't care. I love being like this with him, when neither of us are overthinking. We're just here together in the moment.

He smacks my pussy lightly. "Naughty girl."

The slight sting only has me groaning and spreading my thighs even further apart. For days now, I've felt like I was on the edge of coming. Every look, every touch from Blade. I constantly crave him, and after the test I took this morning, I finally understand why.

He brings his hand to his lips, licking my taste off his fingers. Just the sight has fresh moisture gushing from my body.

He knows what it does to me to see him enjoying my flavor. He smirks at me as he licks his fingers clean. I recognize that look. It's the one that says he wants to draw this out, to spend hours teasing me. But I don't need that right now.

I call his name in a breathy whimper. "Need you. *Please.*"

It's my plea that does it. That has him yanking his pants down to take me right here in the muddy forest. I learned very early on in our marriage that Blade will deny me nothing, especially when I beg him.

He shoves his thick cock inside of my drenched pussy, swearing under his breath the whole time. "Fuck, sweetheart. Why are you always so tight and wet?"

I whimper at the slick friction, at the feeling of being so completely filled by the man that's more than just my husband. He's my best friend. My biggest defender. My soulmate. "You do this to me."

His eyes glitter with something feral and possessive. He slides even deeper, nearly splitting me in two with his massive shaft. "That why you put on this little dress and those running shoes? Needed your man to hunt you down and fuck you right here?"

"Yes! Yes!" I cry out, my nails scrabbling for purchase along his shoulders. They dig deep into his flesh, leaving half-moons.

"Wanted me to take you in the dirt, remind you who owns this sweet, little cunt?" He grunts with each thrust, snapping his hips against mine.

I arch my pelvis up, offering him my body the way he likes. "It's your cunt." It used to embarrass me to say stuff like this during sex, but then I realized just how crazy it makes Blade. How it sets him off.

Just as I expected, he picks up his pace even more. He's going wild over me, his thrusts frantic as he finds my clit. He circles it once, twice, and the third time I'm exploding against him. I scream as I do, letting him and the canopy of trees know just who's making me feel this good.

Blade follows me over the edge, coming with a masculine howl of pride. He's so vocal when we're out here. It's one of the things I love about moments like these, the way he's completely uninhibited and leaning only into his base instincts.

His hot come spills deep into me, and I squeeze him.

"There you go, sweetheart." He brushes a strand of hair from my eyes. "Milk me. Take it all."

His words and the tender gesture have me coming again on his cock. He's so big and so possessive. So demanding in the bedroom and so supportive outside of it. He's everything I could ever hope for in a man, and now he's the father of my child. The thought has tears leaking from my eyes.

"Talk to me," he murmurs, wiping the tears away. He's gotten used to the fact that I tear up easily. He knows I feel everything deeply and sometimes, it all just leaks out. He never gets frustrated or impatient about it. He just holds me through my tears, which thanks to him are mostly happy ones.

I cup his face. His beard is getting longer now. I may have mentioned that big, thick beards are very attractive to me. A razor hasn't touched his face since. He says his electric one quit working, but I know the truth. "You fill my life with so much joy."

He presses a kiss to my palm. "That's my only mission anymore."

"I was thinking you could share the mission," I tell him. He's still inside of me, still hard and ready. He wants me constantly, driven nearly mad with need. We both are, and I love that about our relationship. I never have to question if Blade wants me or finds me beautiful. His continual bulge tells me exactly what he thinks of me.

He scowls, anger sparking in his dark gaze. "I'm not sharing you, and if you ever suggest that again, I'll spank your pretty little ass until it's red and swollen. You belong to me and only me."

I shiver at the suggestion, not because being punished by Blade scares me. No, it sends a fresh rush of moisture to my pussy. Blade loves me fiercely, but he is the alpha in our relationship. I love that about him. The way he never backs down or lets me push him around. "I phrased that wrong."

He makes a hum of contentment in his throat, no doubt feeling the way I'm gushing on his cock again. "Seems we'll need to revisit the spanking idea at some point."

I make a noise of agreement and press a kiss to the hollow of his throat. "I meant that maybe you could divide the mission. Between me and our pups."

"You want another dog?" He asks, eyes crinkling

at the corner. He knows I adore Theodore. He's a delightfully playful pup that keeps me on my toes. He's fiercely loyal to Alvin and Simon. When a coyote tried to come after my precious kitties, he stepped in between them and ran it off with no fear. He's a warrior through and through, just like his strong dad.

If I asked for a dog, I have no doubt that Blade would drop everything to drive me to the adoption center today. He'd encourage me to adopt the whole shelter if it would make me smile. He loves me that much.

I take his hand and put it on my stomach. "This is our newest pup."

His breath comes out in a whoosh, letting me feel every one of his hard planes. Then he's snapping his hips against mine again, body already in motion. "You're giving me babies."

"Yes," I moan as he strokes my pussy with his huge girth. How does it always get better each time? How does he always know just what to do to keep me wet?

"You're making me a daddy." His eyes are filled with a sheen of tears.

I groan my agreement, already thinking of the

way he's going to be inside of me constantly. He's talked of breeding me before, of how he'll be putting his big hands all over my stomach the moment I'm showing. I can't wait for that.

"We made a family," I whisper as he explodes again. His thick come coats my insides and fills me with serenity. He's marked me. He's claimed me and pretty soon, the whole world will know it.

We stay tangled together on the forest floor talking about our future together until the sun finally dips low in the sky. Then Blade helps me to my feet, pausing to adjust my dress so I'm covered again. He hasn't stopped smiling since I told him. I haven't either.

He takes my hand as we walk back toward our cabin. "Daughters. I hope our first six are daughters."

I chuckle, even though the thought that he wants so many children delights me. "Whoa, there, mountain man. Let's see how we feel after this one."

He stops and turns to me. The setting sun is casting a soft, pink glow over the night that makes this moment feel downright magical. "I want to raise daughters just as strong and beautiful as their mama."

My heart squeezes in my chest, and I lean up to

press a gentle kiss to his lips. He's already the best man I know. He'll make an amazing dad, and I can't wait to fill our little cabin with his babies.

Want a bonus scene with Blade and Gwen? Sign up for my weekly newsletter and get the bonus here.

READ NEXT: ENGAGED TO THE MOUNTAIN MAN

Can this innocent princess convince the wild mountain man to claim her curves and his rightful throne?

Rafe

Imagine this: the sexiest voice you've ever heard is on the other end of the phone. She's calling to tell you that you're a prince of some little country in Europe. She's clearly lying, but that voice is the stuff fantasies are made of.

So, I played along with her little scam. Sure, princess, you can visit me. I'll be waiting to pick you up at the airport. Five o'clock sharp. Wouldn't miss it for the world.

Now imagine my surprise when the princess does show up at my mountain cabin. She's madder than a wet cat. What's more, she's insisting that I'm her prince and we're engaged. The joke's on her: this scammer picked the wrong mountain man to play with. Because I sure as hell ain't no prince.

Aurora

Rafael is insufferable! He's supposed to be a prince, my foot. The man looks like he's never had so much as a haircut. He can't possibly be my intended husband. If it weren't for my cousin's schemes, I wouldn't be here convincing this wild mountain man to take his rightful place by my side.

But even after all the time we spend together and the delicious kisses he gives me, I'll still have to choose between my duty and my heart. And I'm not sure which one will win.

If you love a growly alpha with a heart of gold who falls for a curvy princess, it's time to meet Rafe in Engaged to the Mountain Man.

Read Rafe and Aurora's Story

COURAGE COUNTY SERIES

Welcome to Courage County where protective alpha heroes fall for strong curvy women they love and defend. There's NO cheating and NO cliffhangers. Just a sweet, sexy HEA in each book.

Love on the Ranch

Her Alpha Cowboy

Pregnant and alone, Riley has nowhere to go until the alpha cowboy finds her. Will she fall in love with her rescuer?

Her Older Cowboy

Summer is making a baby with her brother's best friend. But he insists on making it the old-fashioned way.

Her Protector Cowboy

Jack will do whatever it takes to protect his curvy woman after their hot one-night stand…then he plans to claim her!

Her Forever Cowboy

Dean is in love with his best friend's widow. When they're stranded together for the night, will he finally tell her how he feels?

Her Dirty Cowboy

The ranch's newest hire also happens to be the woman Adam had a one-night stand with…and she's carrying his baby!

Her Sexy Cowboy

She's a scared runaway with a baby. He's determined to protect them both. But neither of them expected to fall in love.

Her Wild Cowboy

He'll keep his curvy woman safe, even if it means a marriage in name only. But what happens when he wants to make it a real marriage?

Her Wicked Cowboy

One hot night with Jake gave me the best gift of my life: a beautiful baby girl. Will he want us to be a family when I show up on his doorstep a year later?

Courage County Brides

The Cowboy's Bride

The only way out of my horrible life is to become a mail order bride. But will my new cowboy husband be willing to take a chance on love?

The Cowboy's Soulmate

Can a jaded playboy find forever with his curvy mail order bride and her baby? Or will her secret ruin their future?

The Cowboy's Valentine

I'm a grumpy loner cowboy and I like it that way. Until my beautiful mail order bride arrives and suddenly, I want more than a marriage in name only.

The Cowboy's Match

Will this mail order bride matchmaker take a chance on love when she falls for the bearded cowboy who happens to be her VIP client?

The Cowboy's Obsession

Can this stalker cowboy show the curvy schoolteacher that he's the one for her?

The Cowboy's Sweetheart

Rule #1 of becoming a mail order bride: never fall in love with your cowboy groom.

The Cowboy's Angel

Can this cowboy single dad with a baby find love with his new mail order bride?

The Cowboy's Heiress

This innocent heiress is posing as a mail order bride. But what happens when her grumpy cowboy husband discovers who she really is?

Courage County Warriors

Rescue Me

Getting out was hard. Knowing who to trust was easy: my dad's best friend. He's the only man I can count on, but will we be able to keep our hands off each other?

Protect Me

When I need a warrior to protect me, I know just who to turn to: my brother's best friend. But will this grumpy cowboy who's guarding my body break my heart?

Shield Me

When trouble comes for me, I know who to call—my ex-boyfriend's dad. He's the only one who can help. But can I convince this grumpy cowboy to finally claim me?

Courage County Fire & Rescue

The Firefighter's Curvy Nanny

As a single dad firefighter, I was only looking for a quick fling. Then the curvy woman from last night shows up. Turns out, she's my new nanny.

The Firefighter's Secret Baby

After a scorching one-night stand with a sexy firefighter, I realize I'm pregnant...with my brother's best friend's baby.

The Firefighter's Forbidden Fling

I knew a one night stand with my grumpy boss wasn't the best idea...but I didn't think it would lead to anything serious. I definitely didn't think it would lead to a surprise pregnancy with this sexy firefighter.

GET A FREE COWBOY ROMANCE

Get Her Grumpy Cowboy for FREE:
https://www.MiaBrody.com/free-cowboy/

LIKE THIS STORY?

If you enjoyed this story, please post a review about it. Share what you liked or didn't like. It may not seem like much, but reviews are so important for indie authors like me who don't have the backing of a big publishing house.

Of course, you can also share your thoughts with me via email if you'd prefer to reach out that way. My email address is mia @ miabrody.com (remove the spaces). I love hearing from my readers!

ABOUT THE AUTHOR

Mia Brody writes steamy stories about alpha men who fall in love with big, beautiful women. She loves happy endings and every couple she writes will get one!

When she's not writing, Mia is searching for the perfect slice of cheesecake and reading books by her favorite instalove authors.

Keep in touch when you sign up for her newsletter: https://www.MiaBrody.com/news. It's the fastest way to hear about her new releases so you never miss one!